BODY IN THE LAKE

A RITA PATEL MYSTERY

By Catherine Cooper

Oxford eBooks

Chapter

1

"I have touched the highest point of all my greatness, and from that full meridian of my glory, I haste now to my setting."

Cardinal Wolsey in
The Famous History of the Life of King Henry VIII
by Shakespeare

Tuesday July 23rd 2013 (morning)

"High five!" Rita Patel and her friend Priya Shah celebrate changing the last bed and cleaning the last room for the day. After a week of working in the Sundial Bed and Breakfast, they have a system which helps them through the tedium of the morning routine. Rita brings her iPod and dock and they listen to a playlist they compiled for this purpose – Michael Bublé, Emeli Sande, Mylie Cyrus, One Direction, interspersed with 'cheesy' tunes by the Spice Girls and Five, which they secretly like but pretend to disdain. Together they strip and change the beds in the rooms which are all called after flowers – the idea of the owner - now scrunching used sheets and duvet covers into the laundry basket, like experts, now unfolding the new ones which smell of flowers and have sharp folds from the laundry, like envelopes. The girls work as a team, handing corners across the beds and chatting simultaneously. They take it in turns to do the en-suites their least favourite job. While one discovers fresh bathroom horrors, the other dusts the room and deploys the hoover.

It is a tribute to their friendship, which started in junior school and has continued until now, their last year of senior school about to start in a month's time, that the two different characters get on so well. Where Rita is curious and impetuous, Priya is cautious and careful. Where Rita is heedless of risks, Priya is anxious and fearful of consequences she may not be able to control. Rita, who wants to work in a museum, enjoys studying history; Priya hopes to drop history when they get their AS level results and concentrate on the sciences, as she aims to qualify in medicine and work in pathology.

The girls are supposed to be thinking about their 'skills, achievements and experience' as they compose first drafts of their personal statements for their UCAS forms. They anticipate the University phase of their lives with excitement and anxiety ("What will it be like?" asks Priya, whose older sister, Meera, never took that step. "We'll be fine when we get there." is Rita's standard response; she has been to visit her brother Mohal who is in his first year at Hertfordshire Uni and settling in well.) Mr Thatcher, a history teacher at their comprehensive school and also in charge of the school's university applications, has let it be known that he is ready to look at draft personal statements 'any time.' Somehow knowing this has caused writers' block in both pupils.

"Coffee time!" Athena Maitland shouts from downstairs, realising by the silence of the vacuum cleaner that the girls have finished their morning tasks. Rita and Priya gratefully descend the two flights from the top floor which has two bedrooms (known as Rose and Daisy) past the first floor which has three rooms (Daffodil, Bluebell and Poppy) and down to the ground floor, which has one bedroom, arranged for disabled guests in particular, titled Tulip, the guests sitting room, and dining room, and the kitchen.

Rita carries the *Henry* vacuum cleaner cautiously down the steps, steering it expertly around the Stannah lift which juts out at the base of the stairs on the ground floor. Athena had this installed to help frail guests ("Or if you're too inebriated to climb up!" was the unhelpful suggestion of her husband, Edward). Together they stow Henry in the floor length cleaning cupboard in the hall. This takes some care as the cupboard is overfull, being crowded with laundry baskets, croquet equipment, footballs and even a collapsible wheel chair in case guests need it. Athena who owns the B & B, cheerfully calls the cupboard 'the hell hole'. The girls walk gingerly across the tiled hall to the stone floored dining room where Sundial's guests are invited to sit round a large square distressed pine table when they appear for their breakfasts and where Athena is now taking her break.

Rita and Priya have concentrated on the second floor today as two rooms there are occupied; Brian Jackson, an actor, is in Daffodil and a student teacher, Marina Hutchinson, is in the room called Poppy, which is the smallest of the rooms and therefore let out at a cheaper rate. On the top floor, the rooms named Rose and Daisy were occupied at the weekend by couples attending a University reunion dinner; they checked out on Monday morning so the rooms only needed a light dusting today, as did Tulip on the ground floor. This had left more time for the girls to give the floors in the hall and dining room a good clean, hence their reluctance to walk across them now.

Athena has put out a plate of homemade shortbread and a tray bearing a double espresso for herself and two elderflower cordials for the girls. "Ah," she sighs as she sits in one of the pine chairs - there are no two dining chairs the same, Athena having picked them up at junk shops at various times, which adds to the comfortableness of the room. All three settle, with their elbows on the table, glad of the chance to rest for a short while.

"Any sign of them leaving the hospital yet?" Rita asks. The TV in the corner is on with the sound turned down. The picture shows rows of cameras all pointing towards a hospital door.

"No." says Athena smiling. "Look at them all! Would you come out if you knew they were waiting?"

"Good point." says Priya. "Kate will need to get her hair done and everything."

"Prince Charles just went in." Athena adds. "He must be glad to have a grandson."

"Did you see the easel outside the Palace yesterday?" Rita asks their boss, referring to the official notification of the birth of a royal heir in the Lindo Wing of St Mary's hospital, outside which the world's press has been camped waiting for a glimpse of the new arrival.

"Yes, mad isn't it?" Athena replies.

Athena's hair hangs in long curly auburn locks. Although tied back when she is in the kitchen, her hair now tumbles over her shoulders and mingles with silver earrings dangling against the sides of her face. Athena favours 'ethnic' outlets where she buys cotton fabrics and Fairtrade jewellery. She wears a *Great British Bakeoff* pinafore over her blue elephant design top and white Capri pants. She has red canvas wedge-heeled shoes to complete her ensemble.

Rita and Priya, who are opposites in appearance as well as character, are in awe of Athena, not just for her dress sense but for her confidence; Athena is a positive person to be around, Rita and Priya immediately decided when they first met her. Rita is the taller of the friends, with a round face and wavy brown hair; Priya is built to a smaller scale, with fine features, long thin fingers, and straight nearly- black hair which she has a nervous habit of brushing several times a day.

Rita and Priya came to help at Sundial through Jaina, Rita's aunt. She is the secretary at a girl's private school and befriended Athena and her daughter, Morwenna, when the girl joined the sixth form there last year. Jaina soon discovered that Athena was looking for help in the holidays with her Bed and Breakfast, which she runs to help towards

Morwenna's school fees. ("The perils of a second marriage!" she had confided in Jaina, "Edward has to pay university accommodation costs for the children of his first marriage, and he still pays his first wife some maintenance, although goodness knows why, so there's not a lot to go round for Morwenna. And I do want the best for her." Jaina had nodded sympathetically at this; she and her husband, Bandhu, live modestly so that Rita's twin cousins, Shreya and Shona, aged 13, can attend the private school.)

"How's Morwenna doing?" Rita asks their boss as she nibbles at the edge of a shortbread finger.

"She's enjoying it she says." Athena sounds less than convinced, "She seems to be good at it. Selling clothes to pampered rich kids!" she adds with a small laugh, trying to hide her frustration at Morwenna's lack of interest in Sundial and the fact that when she gets back to the garden flat, which forms the basement floor of the house and is where she and her parents live, her daughter tends to flop on the sofa and spend her evenings texting her friends or on Facebook. While her mother provides clean rooms and vegetarian breakfasts (Athena has an interest in Buddhism) Morwenna has a holiday job at Jack Wills and ambition to be chosen for Abercrombie & Fitch.

Rita and Priya exchange glances. They have girls like Morwenna in their year at school, girls they secretly call 'the princesses' on account of their obsession with personal appearance and grooming; they absorb the latest beauty tips and spend their money on beauty products. Priya and Rita do not see themselves as belonging to the princesses, nor, for that matter, to 'the geeks' - the girls who work all the time and enjoy maths club - nor to the 'popular' girls – the girls who go out a lot and talk about clubbing with their boyfriends. Rita and Priya belong to the 'quiet' group (so dubbed by the others); they do not go out in the evening or date boys, their families would not approve.

Their break time over, it is time to tidy the dining room while waiting for Priya's mother to collect them. She is taking the girls to Peterborough for the afternoon to visit her oldest brother, Priya's uncle, Deepak. Athena goes to the kitchen to think about soup. Although Sundial does not cater for lunch or evening meals, Athena always makes her own bread and has a dish available for tired or hungry guests; she likes the Bed and Breakfast to smell of freshly cooked food.

Sundial is in the Knighton area of Leicester, close enough to University accommodation for it to be used by parents and other University visitors. Athena has also developed useful contacts with local theatres and many actors and stage managers have entered and exited the Bed and Breakfast establishment. The house is Edwardian, extends over four storeys, and has a large garden at the back and the front (where the eponymous sundial is to be found in a lawned diamond-shaped island among eight parking spaces). Edward, Athena's husband (his second marriage, her first) and Morwenna's father, looks after the garden when he is not abroad ('Doing my day job' he says) as an intellectual property lawyer with an international client base. Currently he is in Dubai, due back at the weekend.

At the front of the house there are steps down to the garden flat where Athena and her family retire when the needs of the guests allow, and steps up to the front door (wheelchair access is via the kitchen). The black and white tiled hallway, on to which the glazed front door opens, leads to the sitting room, dining room and kitchen as well as the first of the six en-suite rooms which Athena has decorated and themed using Laura Ashley fabrics (Wi-Fi, car parking, tea and coffee making facilities, organic vegetarian breakfast provided).The sitting room is for any guest to relax in; it has sofas, chairs, floor cushions and games, books and DVDs which can be borrowed.

When the telephone rings, Athena is in the kitchen

chopping carrots, near the poster she has put by the sink which says

He who envies others does not attain peace of mind.

Athena calls to the girls to answer the call while she dries her hands and Priya picks up the telephone in the hall .She holds it to her ear as she walks through to the kitchen, anticipating that the call will be Sundial business. "Yes, I'll just get her for you." Rita hears her friend say. She looks quizzically at Priya whose face is raised in a surprised look.

Athena takes the phone from her.

"It's the police" Priya tells her boss as she hands the instrument over. Now it is Athena's turn to produce a puzzled expression.

"What's it about?" hisses Rita to her friend as they move to the dining room to allow Athena privacy "I hope nothing's happened to Edward." she adds, thinking of news stories of people getting into trouble abroad.

"Search me." Priya shrugs. By mutual consent the girls are quiet as they tidy the table in the dining room and straighten the place mats, hoping to overhear Athena's side of the conversation. That is fruitless, however, as all they gather is "I see." "Oh dear." and "Thank you for telling me."

The girls look at each other in puzzlement, hoping their boss will re-appear and provide clarity.

After a few minutes, Athena emerges through the kitchen door, her pinafore removed; she sighs as if bewildered.

"Well" she says, "That's a turn up." Priya and Rita look at her for confirmation. "I'm afraid Brian Jackson won't be coming back to Sundial. It appears he was found dead today," she pauses, "In Abbey Park." Another pause, "In a boat."

Chapter

2

"Be very, very careful what you put in that head because you will never, ever get it out."
                    Attributed to Cardinal, Thomas Wolsey

Tuesday July 23rd 2013 (afternoon)

Rita and Priya are still processing the news as the doorbell rings to announce the arrival of Priya's mother who has used one of the parking spaces and is anxious to set off for Peterborough.

While Priya explains, Rita manages to make sure their boss is sitting down with a cup of tea ('Always tea in a crisis.' her mother, Padma, would say).

"Are you ok?" she asks Athena who is staring ahead at the poster in the dining room which bears the words-

All the happiness there is in the world

Arises from wishing others to be happy.

All the suffering there is in the world

Arises from wishing oneself to be happy.

"Oh yes," Athena breaks out of her paralysis and waves airily at the room, "You girls get off. I'm alright now, I've got used to the shock. You don't expect to take a call like that."

Priya and her mother sit down at the table, too, to show support.

"Did they say how he died?" Rita's investigative antennae are twitching.

"Looks like natural causes, they said." the landlady answers.

"How old was he?" Mrs Shah inquires. Young people don't die of natural causes she is thinking; and not in the open air.

"About mid-fifties would you say Rita?" Athena looks across the table.

"Fifty six." Rita says, "He was telling me only yesterday about his career and how he wanted to keep acting until he was sixty five. He won't get to do that now."

"An actor then?" Mrs Shah again, "One of your theatrical guests?"

"Yes," her daughter answers, "Mr Jackson was in Romeo and Juliet at the Park. He is –was- Friar Laurence."

"Oh dear," Athena groans as she pulls her smart phone from her trouser pocket and starts to thumb through the contacts. "I'd better make sure that the Dragon Company know. They'll need to replace him."

Rita nods, thinking "What about his family? His friends? Would the police notify them?"; she is not sure what the protocol is. The form that guests complete when they check in has their address, contact number, and car registration. Athena does not ask for more details, like next of kin. Why would she? Guests were in and out on a daily basis, there was no need.

While Athena is in the kitchen telephoning the stage manager of the theatre company, Rita goes to consult the folder of guests' forms where Brian Jackson's slim details will be. He gave his address as a house in Grimethorpe ('Sounds like something from Dickens', thinks Rita) which is in Yorkshire, and there were landline and mobile numbers. She notes his car registration too; she is fairly sure she did not see his car at the front of Sundial when they arrived that morning.

Mrs Shah is just saying "When do you think we can go?" thinking of her brother expecting her arrival, when Athena walks back through to the dining room.

"I spoke to Caroline." This is the stage manager for the Dragon Company; Rita and Priya have met her. She is a large woman with bubbly hair and personality. She has strong organising abilities and she often comes to the Bed and Breakfast to stay, when the company are in Leicester, although currently she is staying at another establishment with others from the company. When Dragon were preparing a production in Leicester, Caroline would make herself at home at Sundial, even if she was staying elsewhere, spending the evenings when rehearsals were done in the sitting room with the actors who were guests, playing the board games (Monopoly, Cluedo, Game of Life) with enthusiasm while they put the world to rights helped by Athena's tea and biscuits. (Athena does not encourage alcohol on the premises.)

"She had heard from the police. Apparently one of the Company found him. What a shock. They'll cancel tonight's performance and decide what to do." Athena adds.

"What about Brian's family?" Rita asks. "He told me he shares a house with his mother when he is not touring?" ('How old must she be?' Rita is quietly calculating).

"Yes. The police will let them know." Athena looks around and shakes herself a little, as if rediscovering where she is, like a traveller getting off a plane after a long flight ('The tea must have done the trick' thinks Rita).

"Anyway," Athena says, turning to practicalities, "We'll leave his room as it is. It's possible a family member will call for his things, or they may need a room for a couple of nights. We'll see. Play it by ear. But please," she adds as an afterthought, "Keep this to yourselves. Don't go spreading gossip about this. It might get Sundial a bad name." The other three nod and rise from the pine chairs to go.

"I'll see you girls same time tomorrow. And thanks!" Athena says, back to her brighter self now.

"Let us know if there's anything we can do." This from Priya, while Rita is thinking,

"Let us know if you hear anything else. What can have happened to Brian?"

* * *

As Mrs Shah's car sits at a set of traffic lights on the ring road – a junction with the Uppingham Road, where Rita's parents have their dental practice - Rita is staring idly at the world outside the windows from which they are cut off by glass, air conditioning and George Michael on Heart FM radio. Rita is looking but not seeing, her mind on Brian and possible scenarios. She does not see the children making their way on various forms of transport with their carers. Rita does not take in the buggies and the scooters which propel the under threes, the babies strapped to chests as if being swaddled for work in the fields, or swinging on backs like elephant riders. Rita does not notice the toddlers standing on boards attached to the buggies which Mrs Shah points to as they wait for a green light. "I wish we'd had those when you were little." she says over her shoulder to Priya. "It would have saved a lot of argument from Meera." (Priya's older sister recently married, and, although she lives nearby, Priya's mother misses her presence in the house).

An older couple weave their way uncertainly along the pavement, between the wheeling infants and tree roots which have erupted under the tarmac in places making an extra hazard for them and their frail walking sticks. A group of young men emerges from a burger bar, presumably on their lunch break. They walk with their hands in their pockets, their shoulders hunched.

Rita's brain suddenly emerges from self-hibernation as her attention is caught by a familiar figure. She has seen a couple standing conspiratorially by a wall on the corner of the street and she thinks she recognises one of them. At first she thought the girl was one of the 'princesses' from school, but now she can see it is a woman in her mid-twenties with a strong resemblance to Jennifer Lawrence in the Hunger Games. She has dark hair in a single plait on one side of her head and Rita identifies her as Marina, the student teacher staying at Sundial. Marina has on a long skirt and a thin pink top; she has a white cardigan wrapped round her waist and spreading over her hips. She is shaking her head and looking down as if she is worried.

The man Rita does not recognise; he is tall, early twenties, rangy, pale brown skinned with a fashionable beard on his chin and a woolly hat on his head. The hat accentuates the concerned look in his eyes; he is staring very intently at his companion and Rita thinks this may be what first awoke her attention. The couple seem to be arguing but in whispers, not shouting, and cover their mouths with their hands as they speak. Both have a troubled look and the man suddenly holds out both his hands in an imploring gesture.

"Is this Marina's boyfriend?" Rita is thinking. It's hard to guess from their body language what is going on between them. ('Help, I need subtitles!' Rita thinks.) Their heads are close together now. Are they arguing? Splitting up? As the car pulls away Rita sees the man pull Marina towards him. A lover's tiff perhaps? The intense figures, feelings passing between them like electric current, disappear in the distance behind the car.

Soon Mrs Shah is propelling them along the A47. Priya has nodded off to sleep, her head heavy and rolling, tired after the unaccustomed physical exertion of the morning, and by their early start. Athena generally likes them to be at Sundial by 8.30am to tidy up the sitting room and clear plates from the dining room.

Rita is daydreaming, looking at the blue sky and white clouds, the flat green and yellow fields, the villages in the distance marked by steepled churches. Rita is not paying any more attention to the countryside than she did to the activity in the town. She is recalling her last conversation with Brian Jackson which had been only yesterday, in the gap between his breakfast and his morning run, which he liked to take before he rejoined the Company at about two o'clock to discuss any last minute changes to the play. They had been sitting together at the large square dining table, he with a mug of what Athena calls 'builders' tea', she with a cup of honey and ginger from Athena's herbal range. Rita, who is in the drama club at school ('Make sure you put that on your UCAS form, Rita.' her mother had said) had asked Brian how he got into acting.

"Well lass," he had said in his native, broad, Yorkshire accent, quite unlike the refined received English he put on for the Friar Laurence part, "I like to say I was in the pit, now the people in the pit look up to me."

Rita had looked non-plussed.

"Orchestra pit? Coal mine?" he explained, "I were a miner. Like me Dad before me." Brian had sat back on his chair, expanding his chest. He had thick sliver grey hair, over which he wore a small cap for the play, fine features and a strong nose. He was what people might call 'distinguished looking' Rita thought. His figure was on the lean side – Rita knew he liked to go running most mornings – and he was quite tall, probably about 6 foot two, Rita thought. If you were casting him you would go for aristocrat before peasant, if you just took account of his looks; in fact his greatest success had been as a doctor in a TV soap, a role he occupied for ten years from the end of the 1990s and which made him a household name until an unfortunate (fictional) encounter with an aggrieved patient and an open window in a tower block had brought the character, and Brian's career, crashing down. His descent had been rapid and he had gone from receiving offers to open supermarkets to searching the shelves for offers to keep his food bills down.

"I started in the mine in the eighties. I'd not been long at Grimethorpe Colliery before the strike. Ye'll 'ave 'eard o' that? I expect you did it in history?"

"Mmmn." Rita nodded, "Politics actually. Margaret

Thatcher, the Prime Minister, set out to destroy the miners' power and Arthur Scargill, the miners' leader, played into her hands." Rita parodied the topic for an essay they had discussed at school.

"I were only a bit older than thee." Brian Jackson's Yorkshire accent got thicker as he recalled the past. "I'd just started in t' colliery when th'overtime ban began. I'd been there about a year. Autumn of 1983 that were. Things were never the same again in Grimethorpe - it's where I were born. Where my mother still lives, and me with her when I'm back home." His eyes had moistened wistfully, although all Rita can picture from her politics studies is closed mines, deserted villages, men without jobs or hope. That's what she had seen in the newsreel footage they had studied. Other images sprang to her mind from Billy Elliott - she'd seen the film and the stage show - police brought in from other parts of the country, battles with pickets; it had seemed like the miners were fighting for survival, and lost.

Rita knows there used to be mines in Leicestershire. The clue was in the name of the town - 'Coalville' she thought. The most famous had been at Snibston where in the 1960s the National Coal Board had sunk a drift mine as opposed to a vertical shaft to access the large seam of coal in the area. Snibston had closed in 1983, the year the industrial action started, followed by Leicester South and Whitwick in 1986. Coalville had fallen on hard times but money had been put into regeneration, Rita knew, and she had visited the heritage centre at Snibston with Nayan and Mohal where they looked at the history of mining and the terrible conditions men endured underground.

"It were a grim time. Me Dad and me, on strike. Living on hand outs from t'union and charities. They stopped benefits for strikers and their families. Me Mother trying to get little jobs to keep body and soul together. Soup kitchens. Badges saying 'Coal not Dole' won't feed you. It were dreadful.

But that wasn't the worst part." Rita wondered what would be worse than having no job and no means of support for anyone in the family.

"What was the worst?" she had asked, surreptitiously looking at her watch. Priya, whose turn it was to do the downstairs bathrooms, would want her help with the bedrooms soon.

"The way they turned miner against miner, brother against brother." Brian pauses, real bitterness creeping into his voice.

"You see they broke us up, persuaded those yellow bellies in Nottingham to form another union. So that it were NUM (National Union of Mineworkers) against UDM (Union of Democratic Mineworkers). Sometimes families were split down the middle; some men joined the UDM and went to work in Nottingham; I don't know how they could… People didn't speak for years after, still don't speak, not to scabs, not to turncoats." Rita could see Mr Jackson's jaw tighten in stubbornness as he spoke.

"And the acting?" she reminded him.

"Oh aye, lass,sorry," he had apologised, looking into his mug to appraise how much tea there was left, "So after a twelve month we went back to work. Colliery band playing. The women put carnations at the pit as a welcome. But it were never the same. Collieries closed left right and centre. Arthur Scargill had been right. Men out of work. Nay jobs to go to. This was the 1980s. There were no jobs. This so-called recession we've just been through, believe me things were a lot worse then. So when I got my cards I signed on with various agencies, more hopeful than expecting like, and one lass put me on to a modelling job. I were not bad looking in them days." he had puffed out his chest and smiled, the years peeling away as he did so. (Recalling how proud he had looked only the day before made Rita feel very sad.)

"Turned out I weren't bad at the modelling lark." Brian

had continued. Seeing Rita's sceptical looked he leaned across the table to add,

"All above board, clothes and cars and that." Rita had nodded appreciatively. "I got a loan to help with the modelling, from one those enterprise companies they set up to try to help us. Lots of the women got help that way – including me Mam- she set up a cake business. Sold her ginger parkin all over the country. Me Dad never worked again, mind – bad lungs you see - died of emphysema in the nineties." He had paused to reflect, just as Priya had appeared round the door with a dust pan in her hand and an inquiring expression on her face.

As Rita stood to go, Brian finished his story. "So modelling led to acting. I got meself part time jobs and studied in London. I acted all over the country. Got a bit of TV - some small parts in The Bill and Midsummer Murders - and then my big break as Doctor Page. Maybe you've seen the repeats? Those were the glory years. Steady money, other parts coming in. Trouble is it doesn't last. But at least I'm doing something I love. And I'm not underground all day!" he finished, as Rita waved and left the room. That was the last time she had seen him she reflected soberly.

* * *

"Poor Brian," Rita says, seeing her friend stirring awake as Mrs Shah, disobeying the insistent suggestions of the sat-nav which, like a lost Dalek, keeps ordering her to 'RECALIBRATE') negotiates her way round the ring roads of Peterborough and homes in on Deepak's new flat, which is close to the centre, near ASDA. There are brown road signs to indicate the Cathedral and Priya's mother plans to encourage the girls to visit it while she is admiring her brother's latest property acquisition, and hearing about his progress in the buy-to-let market ('Things are very buoyant thanks to the last Government's immigration policy; all those entrants from Eastern Europe wanting places to stay.' he had told her on the phone.) As she approaches, Mrs Shah can see there have been changes since the last time she visited the City; several Polish supermarkets have sprung up on the roads leading into the centre and her brother has told her the Catholic churches in the area are very busy, causing parking problems on Saturday evenings and Sunday mornings.

Rita is scrolling through twitter on her phone. Already there are several messages about Brian, so the news is spreading, she thinks.

"RIP Brian. Lovely Guy."

"So sad about Brian. Love to his family."

"Just heard the guy who played Dr Page has died. Great shame."

Seeing that Priya is now fully awake Rita asks "Do you know who else died in Abbey Park?"

"No." says Priya looking sideways, "But I think you're going to tell me." She rolls her large brown eyes and rummages in her bag for her comb so she can start on combing out her long dark hair. Her mother glances disapprovingly at her through the rear view mirror; she dislikes this habit Priya has developed.

"Cardinal Wolsey." Rita says triumphantly. Priya shrugs; she is looking forward to giving up history. Having her heart set on forensic medicine means she will concentrate on the sciences and for her the easy part of the UCAS personal statement is to 'outline your ambitions when you finish the course'. (Her father is less sure this is a wise choice. "Too much Silent Witness" he says "It's not like Emelia Fox in real life.") But Priya knows this. She has been to Sheffield University to look round the faculty and learn more about their course. She has also discussed pathology with Leicester University students at an open day. If only she can get an offer of a place, she thinks anxiously.

"Tell me more." Priya reluctantly encourages Rita as she starts to comb her hair.

"You remember." Rita says, "Mr Thatcher used to say 'He saved his life by dying at Leicester.'"

"Well, no, I don't, but go on." Priya prompts.

"He was supposed to arrange the annulment of Henry VIII's marriage to Katharine of Aragon, his first wife, you must remember that bit? So that Henry could marry Anne Boleyn? But he messed up. So Henry had him arrested for treason. On his way back to London from Yorkshire he stopped at the Abbey at Leicester – the Abbey was near the river, where the park is now - and died there. So the king never got to try him and execute him."

"If it's Henry VIII, I'm surprised the Abbey was still here." says Priya, "Didn't Henry dissolve all the monasteries?"

"Well that was a few years later. After Wolsey. Like in those long books that win the prizes, the ones Mr Thatcher's always telling us to read." Rita says, waving her hands as if that would help her memory.

"'Wolf Hall' and 'Bring Up the Bodies'?" says Priya, who has dipped into them but not got far.

"Yeah. Wolsey looked into the corruption at the monasteries and closed a few small ones but dissolution only got going under his successor, Thomas Cromwell."

"How come you remember all this?" says Mrs Shah from the front of the car as they pass through the inner city – they are close to their destination now, as signified by the Victorian terraces interspersed with shops, some of which have signs in Eastern European and Asian languages. She is looking forward to seeing Deepak's penthouse at the top of the block of flats she can see approaching.

"I've done some notes on Wolsey, in case I need a topic to discuss at any University interview, if I get asked for one." Rita pats her Cath Kidston bag where her iPad rests, safely storing her notes. Priya thinks anyone as dedicated as her friend is bound to get offers from Universities.

"I'll tell you another coincidence." Priya can sense one of her friend's obsessions coming on. Surely Rita is not going to try to investigate Brian Jackson's death is she?

"Wolsey, when he was in trouble, went to the north to live, in Yorkshire. In Cawood to be precise. And Brian was from Yorkshire!"

Chapter

3

"Oh how wretched is that poor man who hangs on prince's favours."

Character of Cardinal Wolsey in
The Famous History of the Life of King Henry VIII
by Shakespeare

Wednesday July 24th 2013

The next day Rita and Priya are dropped at Sundial at 8.30am, as usual, by their respective fathers, who then drive to their work. Rita's father is a dentist with his own practice, Priya's father sells computers and computer equipment, sometimes working from home but often travelling round the country. Today he is taking the M69 to Coventry. Athena is in the kitchen scrambling eggs for the new guest in Daisy, who, she tells the girls, is Professor Rees, an archivist from a Welsh University who is studying some material held locally. Rita makes a mental note to try to talk to the guest who may have useful tips on her personal statement.

"How was Peterborough?" Athena asks.

"Great thanks." As they go to the cupboard known as the 'hell hole' to take out tabards to wear for their cleaning role, Rita recalls the enclosed space of the Close surrounding Peterborough Cathedral, which they had visited the previous day; the buildings were huddled together for practicality and protection and it was possible to project on to them ideas of gossip and intrigue like those Rita enjoyed in Trollope's Barchester Chronicles. The low buildings in soft yellow brick seemed to have windows like eyes and had conveyed the sensation of being watched as they had come through the stone gate, leaving behind the modern, teeming square and shopping streets and stepping into this older, quieter, more sedate world.

The Cathedral overwhelmed with its size, and the symbolism, which was everywhere, made Rita feel like she was walking through a giant puzzle or computer game. There was an overawing amount of imagery to take in and Rita had found she needed to be selective as to what to attend to as they strolled through. Among the many monuments, though, her delight was in finding ("You knew that was there, didn't you?" said Priya) the tomb of Katharine of Aragon. Rita was pleased to see fresh flowers had been placed by it – so she was not forgotten then, not overlaid by Henry's later wives. She, after all, had seemed to behave with dignity throughout, Rita thought, especially when Henry convened a court to decide if his marriage was valid; she had knelt before the King, Rita remembered reading "If I have done anything amiss I am willing to be put away in shame." she had said. It was not her fault that her first husband died. She and Henry had been happy, so far as you could tell, when they first married. It was her failure to produce a living son (she had one but he died as a baby), Rita had mused as she looked at the monument, and presumably her fading charms as she grew older, that drove Henry into the arms of Anne Boleyn who played her cards well and secured marriage and the fortunes of her Boleyn family, at least for a time.

Bound up with their love story was the decline and fall of his Grace the Cardinal. How did Wolsey rise so high, from humble beginnings to be a Cardinal? Was he just able and ambitious? Rita thought she needed to check that out. Why was he not able to secure the annulment Henry wanted so badly? Did he think Henry would tire of the idea if he played for time? Or that Anne or the King would give in and sleep together anyway? She had read that when he could not get the annulment, Wolsey plotted to remove Anne from the country. Wolsey had sensed that if the Pope did not side with the King there would be trouble ("Ruin, infamy and subversion" as he put it). He had been right; the Church had changed direction after his death and the King assumed power over the state and the Church. Wolsey's property was forfeited as result of his alleged treason - someone (probably the King?) benefited from his downfall.

As the girls sat in the refectory tea room, sipping hot chocolate and waiting for Mrs Shah to text that she was ready for their rendezvous, Priya was playing *Candy Crush* on her phone and Rita was checking her iPad notes. Wolsey was ill when he decided to stop-over at Leicester. Rita wonders if that itself is suspicious. Could he have been poisoned, or even taken poison himself? Would he have done that rather than face the disgrace of a trial?

Wolsey died in 1530 and the Abbey was dissolved eight years later. Rita had read from the website that a manor house was built on the Abbey's land, ruins of which can be seen in the park; the remains of the Abbey were not examined and the site analysed until the 1930s, when the land came into the hands of the Town Council. It was the architect, William Bedingfield, who had carried out some archaeological excavations and laid out the low walls which now delineate the lines of the main rooms of the monastery. The ruins were used by the University for training archaeologists, Rita had read. It was among these walls that the Dragon Company were currently performing their play. Would they get a substitute for the Friar Laurence part? Rita speculated to herself. Presumably they have understudies for unfortunate eventualities?

Back in the car after Mrs Shah had taken tea with her brother, Rita took up the notes she had made on her iPad again. Ah yes, when Wolsey entered the monastery of St Mary de Pratis (which means St Mary of the Meadows she had found out), an Augustinian Abbey established in the twelfth century at Leicester, he was very ill with dysentery. That must be what finished him off, that and knowing he had lost the King's favour, Rita thought. Wolsey died 29th November 1530. Even after this, she read, Henry thought he could marry Anne and avoid a rift with the Pope but that idea faded when Thomas Moore, who opposed a breach with Rome, had to resign and was replaced by Thomas Cromwell - both he and the Archbishop of Canterbury, Thomas Cranmer – ('Too many people called Thomas!' Rita thinks), were probably influenced by the writings of Martin Luther and arranged a divorce which the Pope opposed. Cromwell drew up the Act of Supremacy making Henry head of the Church of England and this became law in 1534.

Peterborough Cathedral had been an Abbey too. They had seen displays about the life of the monks. It had been a Benedictine Abbey founded in 966. The Church survived on dissolution by being adopted as the Cathedral for the area. It was dedicated to three saints, Saint Peter ('The one with the keys' Rita thinks), Saint Paul (the one who wrote the letters) and Saint Andrew (one of the fishermen). The current building was begun in 1118.

Now as she and Priya are clad in their tabards and going about their daily cleaning tasks, Rita thinks about the routines of the monks' lives. They kept regular hours of worship, rising early and working in the monastery or in the fields or gardens when they were not at their devotions. They were all men, of course, any women would be living in different religious houses. Some of the issues Wolsey and Thomas Cromwell uncovered were to do with bad behaviour by the monks and nuns.

When the monasteries were dissolved, Rita recalls from her reading, a lot more was lost than just religious houses. The Abbeys were business centres, organising trade in local produce, and they attracted a lot of tourists because of the relics they kept. Pilgrimages became fashionable, which boosted the local economy. Abbeys even helped the population to regulate their lives, making sure everyone was aware of the different parts of the church year and also, because they prayed at certain times, they were the first institutions to have clocks. So the lives of ordinary people as well as the lives of the monks would have been upset by the dissolution, the heart taken out of the community and a source of income and financial stability lost.

The Abbeys were very wealthy and no doubt the Abbotts had been tempted towards corrupt and immoral behaviour which they could get away with as they were their own judges, Rita thinks. In Leicester the Abbey had controlled about 40 churches in the county and over a dozen in surrounding counties. The Abbey held manors in Leicestershire and two in Lancashire. Many Abbeys owned mining and related drainage rights over their lands and charged people for the privilege of exercising them; the rents were payable to the King after dissolution.

The first abbot at the Abbey in Leicester was appointed in 1143 and the last in 1538, although he was probably an appointee of Thomas Cromwell, Rita thinks, since he surrendered the Abbey and was well rewarded. On the site there had been a Church, cloister, chapter house and guest hall, according to the layout of the ruins. There were also kitchens, an infirmary and dormitory. It was one of 29 monasteries in Leicestershire, showing how dominant was the power of the monasteries at one time.

As they are cleaning the room called Poppy, currently occupied by the student teacher, Marina, who is out on her course at the University, Athena comes to see them.

"Hi girls. Good job." she says encouragingly, pushing some of her tumbling auburn hair behind on ear. Breakfast is over for the day so her thoughts are turning to what dish to make for later.

"Brian's mother phoned, poor woman. She must be

in shock. It's not like he was ill or anything. Anyway, she sounded very composed. She wants us to box up his things so they can be fetched at a later time." she tells the girls.

"Don't the police want to look in his room?" Rita asks. ('Isn't that what they do on TV?' she thinks.)

"Oh no," says Athena. "They're not treating this as suspicious. It looks like maybe he had a heart attack?" her voice goes up at the end of her sentence – a statement and a question in one.

"Was he old enough for one?" says Priya, then realises that is a foolish statement, didn't that young footballer nearly die of heart failure a couple of years ago?

"Who knows what state any of us is in." says Athena, "Although Brian did take care of himself. He used to go out running, didn't he? Well, we never know what's going to happen do we?" she adds.

"I've brought up some boxes." Athena produces them from the doorway "I wondered if you would do that for me while I'm at the supermarket?"

Rita and Priya look at each other. Pack up a dead man's belongings? But it's what Athena wants, so "OK" they say and "We'll do it after we finish cleaning in Poppy."

"Great," says Athena. "I'll be back in about an hour." And she turns to disappear, relieved to be going.

The girls know that 'an hour' means two or more as Athena will probably stop for a coffee before, or after, shopping and may well bump into a friend there which will make the expedition longer.

"That's fine." says Rita. Priya is coming back to her house later, after they have been to the Central Library in the town centre, a trip which Rita is planning and of which Priya is currently unaware. Rita plans to get Mohal, her brother, who has a summer job as a library assistant, to help her trace some information about Brian.

Athena has not quite gone. She returns to add, "Oh,

and Caroline, the stage manager for Dragon, is calling in tomorrow with some of the company. I think they are at a bit of a loss as to what to do. I said we'd give them coffee in the sitting room. You don't mind helping?"

"Of course not." says Priya. Rita thinks this may be a chance to find out more about what happened.

Half an hour later and Rita and Priya are standing in Daffodil, until recently Brian's room, on the first floor. It is light with large picture windows – original when Athena bought the house but now replacement double glazed units – and a high ceiling. The bed in the centre has a yellow and blue Laura Ashley bed spread to match the curtains and the cushions. The quilt cover and bed sheets are the ubiquitous white used throughout the establishment. A pale blue throw lies limply over the armchair by the window. There is a small cupboard in walnut brown either side of the bed, which has a walnut-effect head board. The chest of drawers and wardrobe are also walnut coloured and there is a mirror on top of the drawers. A pale blue rug rests on the beige carpet. There is a step up into the bathroom which has a lower ceiling, shower, sink and heated towel rail. The tiles are white with a border in yellow and blue. Athena had left Brian a vase of daffodils on the window sill to brighten the room.

Unable to bring themselves immediately to open the drawers and cupboards and touch any of Brian Jackson's possessions, Rita and Priya start by picking up what they can from the surfaces. As they collect up his books – mainly paperbacks from charity shops – Gone Girl, The Slap, Skippy Dies – but also some plays, a dictionary and a book of quotations – Rita has an disquieting feeling that Brian is going to walk into the room at any moment saying 'Ay up. What are you lasses up to?' It makes the back of her neck prickle to think about it. On the iPod Robbie Williams is singing Angels, which is not helping to lighten the atmosphere. Rita can sense that Priya too is feeling melancholy. Her friend sinks down on the bed, then stands up again quickly. It feels wrong to make themselves comfortable here.

"Look, he isn't coming back." Rita voices both their fears. "And it is sad, but there's nothing we can do…"

"Yeah" says Priya "At least we can do this. It's what his family wants."

So, having packed Brian's alarm clock, electric razor and the contents of his wash bag, which includes a throat spray, they clear away two spoons, a used mug (tea dregs in the bottom judging by the tea bag in the bin) and two dirty glasses,

"Looks like these were used for the red wine?" Rita remarks to Priya. There is a bottle which was also in the waste bin and is now in the recycling waste bag. Rita takes a deep breath and opens the wardrobe door. It is poignant to look at the clothes which once hung on a person and now hang lifeless on a rail, shapeless and meaningless, empty shells. Rita folds the trousers – she has two brothers, one older (Mohal) and one younger (Nayan) so she feels more accustomed to this task than Priya who only has an older sister. Priya folds the t-shirts and places them reverently in one of the boxes, together with one jumper and one tie. Rita puts the trousers on top and then Brian's jacket.

Rita says, "I wonder what he was wearing when he was found?"

"When did he go out?" Priya asks, "We didn't see him when we arrived yesterday so he must have gone out early?"

"S'pose," says Rita, "Odd though, because once a play has started he usually has a lie-in. 'Saves me energy' he'd say. We often saw him go out about 12 didn't we?"

"Yeah." Priya has found the ubiquitous black desert boots that Brian always wore and added them to the pile. "Sometimes he'd let us clean his room while he made himself a late breakfast downstairs. Athena'd let him do some toast in the kitchen."

"So he must have gone out early." As Rita speaks, Priya sees her friend has her far away, detecting, expression in her face.

"Who knows what actors like to wear anyway!" Priya says.

"Yeh, surprised we haven't found a cravat!" the girls laugh together, glad to have an excuse to lighten the mood and relieve the tension.

Next, Rita swallows hard and opens the top drawer of the chest. Instead of the underwear she anticipated ('I expect I'll have to touch that as well.' she had thought) there were papers and magazines – mail Brian had received, and some scripts for plays with various parts highlighted. Rita knows that actors often learn parts for auditions, She has overheard members of the company in the guest rooms, pacing up and down, practising delivery in a variety of accents and pitches. How nerve- wracking it must be to put themselves on the line like that, to have their appearance and demeanour judged, to face rejection on a regular basis. Once an actor had confided in her "I don't know why we bother to learn parts for these things, Very often they want a particular look. So, as soon as you appear you might hear someone whisper 'Too tall.' Or 'too short.'" These were factors outside the actor's control Rita had thought.

The drawer also contains magazines of the kind Rita had seen on the top shelf in WH Smith and which she was fairly sure her younger brother Nayan kept under his mattress. She gingerly picks up the naked ladies to go into the box.

"Surely his family won't want these?" Priya thoughtfully says.

"No I guess not." says Rita, "Good point."

So the ladies go into the recycling bag. The post includes bills for a property in Grimethorpe, the one in Alexandra Terrace which Brian had put down as his home address on the Sundial registration form. Someone else would need to pay these now, Rita thinks. There are also property details from estate agents for flats in Doncaster. Had Brian been planning to move out of the house he shared with his mother when he wasn't on the road? Beneath these were letters from firms of solicitors. Rita sinks on to the bed to read them, to Priya's consternation.

"You can't read his letters!"

"Why not, he won't mind now. And there might be a clue here." Rita says distractedly, unconcerned.

"Clue to what?" Priya hisses. "Nothing happened. It was natural causes!"

"Yes, but why did he have a heart attack? It wasn't Athena's breakfasts – they are well-balanced vegetarian fare and her bread's organic." she adds, quoting Athena's promotional literature.

Priya throws her hands up in the air in a gesture of mock despair and opens the other drawers while Rita reads. Priya finds socks, a belt and some boxer shorts, which she hurriedly throws in to the box. Then she moves to the cupboards beside the bed. There is just a Gideon Bible in the one on the left. On top of the one on the right is a spectacles case. Priya opens this but it is empty. It should contain his reading glasses she thinks. Priya knows this because the girls have seen him reading the paper at breakfast on previous visits, the glasses perched on the end of his nose so he can look over them at what is happening in the room. "No reading glasses." she says to Rita, who is engrossed.

"Mmmn Look at this!" she lifts up one of the letters, from a firm called Willis and Moon in Leeds. Priya is not sure she wants to be involved in looking at Brian's correspondence.

"Last month he was changing his will. I wonder that he was up to." Rita observes.

"Doesn't the letter say?" Priya indulges her friend.

"You know what these lawyers are like, it's hard to follow. 'We are in receipt of your instructions blah blah… Revert to you with a draft to reflect your instructions.'" Rita quotes "All the rest is blurb – about who is in charge and how to make a complaint." she adds.

"Well I think that's everything," says Priya, "There is nothing in this cupboard" indicating the one on the right, "So we can leave the boxes for Athena and just clean in here."

"Guess so." says Rita, reluctant to think of leaving the room now, as if Brian is somehow still alive while they clean and explore his possessions.

"Here's a letter from another firm of solicitors – Haddon and Haddon in Harrogate. Looks like Brian was a beneficiary under a will. It is headed 'In the matter of William Frederick Jackson, deceased. I am writing to inform you blah blah' – Golly, look – 'in the region of £500,000 once all duties, taxes and our fees have been paid…' Brian was rich!"

"Or going to be." Priya is interested now. "What's the date on the letter?"

"It's last month." Rita explains, then, "Oh and another letter from Willis and Moon in Leeds. He was getting divorced. No, he was divorced. Decree," Rita hesitates, unsure how to pronounce the Latin word in the letter, she opts to spell it out, "A decree N-I-S-I, whatever that means." she says. "Given just last week."

"OMG! How did he have time to be in a play when he was dealing with all these lawyers?" Priya says.

"He obviously had a lot on his mind", Rita agrees, putting the letters in the box, and thinking 'maybe this led his heart attack?'

By the time Athena arrives back at Sundial they have stripped and changed the bed, emptied the bins and hoovered the room. As an afterthought, Rita has thrown away the daffodils- they were creating a funereal atmosphere she thought.

Chapter

4

"Two households, both alike in dignity, in fair Verona, where we lay our scene, from ancient grudge to new mutiny, where civil blood makes civil hands unclean."

Chorus, *Romeo and Juliet*,
by Shakespeare

Thursday 26th July 2013

The company gather in the sitting room the next day. Rita and Priya join them. Athena has provided homemade shortbread which the girls hand out. Jacob, a young black actor with dreadlocks and a deep voice which resonates across the room, takes charge in distributing the coffee. He declines a proffered biscuit on the grounds that he is diabetic, and several of the thin young actresses refuse because of their figures. Judith, an older woman, gratefully tucks in as do Rita and Priya, hungry after their cleaning work. They have brought cartons of apple juice which they pierce with straws as they take their places among the interspersed actors. Athena's cushions, bearing various words - (LIFE, LOVE, HOPE, PEACE, LAUGH) - languish incongruously on sofas and floors as if no one wants to embrace those concepts today.

As well as the stage manager, there are three young women and four young men in the company, plus the older lady, Judith, and Michael, in his mid-thirties. The room is full and although the day is sunny the tall ferns on the window sill, and the bodies camped on the window seats, obscure the light and cast unaccustomed shadows. The actors have been introduced to Rita and Priya; some they met during the company's visit to Leicester in the May half term when they had all ended up playing a hilarious game of croquet on the lawn at the back of Sundial at which the girls had cheated and the boys pretended to be outraged. Brian had taken part in that game Rita recalls, laughing and joking with them all. Other guests had looked on from the terrace with a mixture of disdain and envy. The actors knew how to put on a show.

The two young women sprawling at either end of the battered leather sofa, one with fine ginger hair tied today in two plaits, which Rita thinks gives her a Viking look, the other with short dark hair and a fashionable headband, are Rachel and Caris. They were here for the May week and shared the bedroom on the top floor . Rachel sports a Parka coat over her long black top and jeans; she sits with the coat huddled on her lap as if for comfort. Caris has favoured a vintage floor length button through dress with knee length boots which she crosses and re-crosses at the ankles nervously as she stares out of the window. Between them is a man in his mid-thirties, short and muscular looking, with stubby dark hair and a t-shirt with a Pink Floyd album cover on it; this is Michael. He looks like a younger version of Ross Kemp, in khaki combats and trainers. He is the only man not clad in black. Judith, the older actress, is heavily built ('Juliet's nurse perhaps?' thinks Rita) and is sitting in one of the arm chairs. She wears leggings under a voluminous turquoise kaftan and has matching art deco earrings which complete her bohemian appearance.

"Kind of you to put this on for us." the deep tones of Caroline the stage manager address Athena from the other arm chair where she is perched on the arm, somehow framing a bearded young male actor who sits in the chair wearing a black t-shirt and narrow black jeans descending into desert boots, looking thin and frail by comparison with Caroline's robust appearance.

"We've not been sure what to do with ourselves." this from

Alicia, a young woman with a pale complexion and fair hair piled on her head, who is sitting on cushions on the floor, her legs bent under her as if she is using the time to practice yoga. Alicia is wearing all black - shorts over tights with a shawl wrapped round her top to complete the mourning effect.

"Yes, ever since Ash found Brian," Caroline indicates the tall lean young man next to her. Rita recognises him now; this is the person Marina was meeting (or arguing with?) when Rita saw her from the car, the day before yesterday. Rita speculates as to who he might play. Romeo perhaps, or Tybalt?

"Is there any news on what happened to Brian?" Rita cannot resist asking.

Caroline speaks for the group "Not really, they are doing a post mortem as it's an unexplained death but they think heart attack. Hopefully it was quick. They'll do a toxicology check as well but I can't believe Brian took anything, he wasn't the kind to dabble in drugs."

"What about his family?" Priya addresses Athena.

"His wife – ex-wife I should say – has been contacted I believe. He had a son with her, so they may call in some time to see where it happened so to speak. She – Jan – stayed here before, I don't know if you remember her? His mother said she'll organise the funeral. She sounded very practical. I doubt his first wife will come, from what I gather things were difficult between them, but he has another son from that marriage so maybe they will get in touch."

Rita thinks "Complicated history, Brian, I wonder how you were changing your will?"

Out loud Rita says "He was in a boat?" she is addressing Ash. Priya shoots her a sharp look that says – these people are grieving! Leave them be!

"Yeah," the reply comes. Ash has a Scottish accent, black clothes and black boots which make him recede further into the chair as Rita looks at him. "I was just passing by the lake, the pedaloes were tied up – ye know how they are?"

Rita nods. She has been to Abbey Park, which is close to the City Centre, with her family. As well as the low walls which show the layout of the Abbey there are well-laid out gardens for walks, and a café with a statue of Cardinal Wolsey beside it - she makes a mental note to remind Priya of this. Wolsey planned to be buried in Westminster Abbey and had a black marble sarcophagus already prepared. Being buried in the Abbey at Leicester was not part of his plans. The River Soar flows by the park and there is also a lake, part of which is used for model boats and part is given over to pedaloes in the school holidays. These can be hired for half an hour and hot summer days are pierced by squeals and shouts of excitement as young people attempt to navigate around the lake. The water is not very deep, Rita thinks, but she has never had occasion to find out. The boats are moored at one end when not in use.

"What time was this?" Rita asks as Priya makes a sucking noise as if of disapproval, through the straw in her carton.

"About 8 i' the morning," Ash says, "There wasn't anybody else around. I went early to check the lighting, we'd had a few issues w'it the night before."

('Oh' thinks Rita, 'So Ash is not actually in the play. He's backstage.')

"Ash is our Assistant Stage Manager - electrician and general handyman." Caroline offers by way of explanation, "I don't know how we'd manage without him." And she gives him a reassuring smile which he modestly deflects.

"He looked very peaceful." Ash goes on, leaning forward into the room, seeing a need to tell his story. "Like he was sleeping in the boat."

"Were his clothes wet?" Rita wants to know. "He hadn't been in the water as far as you could tell?"

"Oh, nay," Ash juts his chin down as if this had not

occurred to him before. "I called to him and shook him, thinking he was asleep. Come to think of it he was a wee bit damp - clammy I suppose - but I couldn't rouse him. I realised he was probably dead. I didn'a know what to do so I just dialled 999. By the time the police arrived a park keeper had turned up so at least I had some company. He shook him in case he was drunk or something like that. The keeper said it's happened before. People the worse for wear sleeping it off in the boats. But I'm afraid poor Brian was gone…" he takes a sip from his china mug and stares ahead of him.

"So unexpected." Judith from her chair chips in. There are murmured voices of assent. "He gave a good performance on Monday night."

"Oh yes," Michael agrees from the sofa.

"What was he wearing?" Rita asks Ash.

Someone in the window seats – possibly Anton, says "A monk's outfit, he was Father Laurence!" before realising Rita was not referring to his stage outfit.

"He'd changed." Ash explains, "He was in joggers and a sweat shirt. Like he was out for one of his runs. He had his glasses on. They fell off when I shook him." He shudders at the memory.

"So he came back to Sundial after the play? Did anyone see him on Monday night or Tuesday morning?" Priya rolls her eyes at Rita's continued questioning and wishes she had her comb with her so she can address her hair during the discussion, which she would find soothing.

Athena, from the faded yellow chintz sofa, contributes, "He would usually stay out late after a performance. He used to say he needed time to wind down. He had a key to the front door – all the guests do. I thought I heard him come in around 11 pm – I was in my flat, meditating, so I looked out of my curtains, you can see the steps up to the house from my flat - and I saw two pairs of feet. Brian's and a woman's. Then in the morning he didn't appear for breakfast so at first

I assumed he was having a lie-in. He often did. When he hadn't surfaced I checked his room and found he had gone out already."

"Did anyone see him after the performance? See him leave the Park?" Rita again.

"Who was last to see him alive you mean?" this from Alicia on the floor who then bursts into tears sobbing, "Poor Brian!" Rachel uncurls from the sofa and stoops to put an arm round her.

Caroline speaks. "After the curtain call – it was a decent-sized audience I thought – he went to the men's changing area."

"Yes, Um." Aaran, sharing a window seat with Jacob, speaks quietly into the room which is hushed now Alicia's outburst has ended; he pushes his spectacles onto the bridge of his nose as he continues, "I saw him when he was getting changed. He said he was meeting someone at a bar. Maybe I was the last to see him."

('Except for the person Brian went to meet,' thinks Rita. 'Who was that?')

The conversation turns to performances they have seen Brian give. Older cast members reminisce about his TV appearances. More recently he had been critically acclaimed for his performance of Polonius in a northern touring company's production of Hamlet.

"Good job nobody noticed his black eye." Judith says, surprising everyone. She recounts how she was playing Queen Gertrude in the Hamlet production and had come across Brian in animated conversation in the Arndale Centre in Doncaster. The other protagonist looked about Brian's age but had close-cropped grey hair and was 'less well preserved' in Judith's phrase. She heard raised voices, exchanged words like 'Judas' and 'betrayer' and phrases like "You did all right for yourself." being bandied about and many unprintable ones she adds. "Anyway it attracted the attention of the security guards but before they could defuse the situation a blow had been struck and Brian got a black eye for his pains. It was very uncharacteristic" Judith says, "It was so unlike his television persona; anyone who saw the fight would have been amazed!"

"I'm surprised it didn't make the papers." Athena says.

"Lucky there were no papparazzi around that day." Caroline agrees.

"Did Brian explain what it was about?" this from Aaran.

"Something from the past he said. Ancient history. Old battles. We were glad to move on to Oxford. No fights there. They kill you with words." Judith concluded.

Rita recalls from the newspaper archives she was able to access with Mohal's help in the Central library yesterday ("Why do we have to come here?" Priya had asked. "What are you looking for?") that Brian had performed some Shakespeare at Oxford Castle – a building she and Priya had caught a glimpse of when they went to the applications seminar which Mr Thatcher had signed them up for. Brian also had reviews for parts in the York Mystery Plays ('What are those?' Priya wanted to know.) There were various cuttings about his role as Dr Page, and his character's sudden demise which seemed to take the press by surprise. The celebrity pages featured his glamorous (second) wedding to Jan, this must have been at the height of his success in the TV soap. The birth of their son, William, was covered by Hello magazine, so he must have been doing well at that time. Rita had made a note to track down Brian's birth and marriage certificates and those of his parents - from their conversation it had sounded like Brian was very young when he first married. How long had that lasted once he left the colliery and took up acting, she had wondered?

"What are mystery plays?" Priya now asks Judith as the subject has come up. She explains that they are traditional plays from medieval times, often performed by the workers' guilds (mystery relating to the Latin for occupation or craft but also sometimes called miracle plays). The guilds got involved when the Pope of the day banned the clergy from taking part. The plays relate to scenes from the Bible she tells Priya. Judith says they were performed in cycles every few years, and the most well-known are those of York and Chester. Traditionally the local people would have performed them, now they were a mixture of professional and amateur players. Some of the actors start to mimic rural accents and repeat some of the lines from the plays. Their enthusiasm and jollity lightens the mood in the room.

As the group are leaving, Rita notices out of the corner of her eye the figure of Morwenna, Athena's daughter, ethereally floating across the hall to the kitchen. She must have a day off Rita thinks as she manages to manoeuvre next to Aaran, waylaying him in the tiled hallway where they can see each other in the long mirrors which adorn the walls.

"You saw Brian when he was changing after the play on Monday night. Do you remember what he changed into – what he was wearing that night?"

Aaran screws up his eyes, trying to picture what he saw. "That's a toughie" he says, "No one wants to stare at a bloke in the changing area. Definitely a shirt, though, I remember him doing up the buttons, jeans and a jacket, I think."

* * *

As Athena sees the actors off the premises, Rita and Priya gather up the mugs and take them through to the kitchen. Morwenna is furtively ferreting in the fridge when they enter and hastily closes the door.

"Hi." the girls greet each other warily. "I was just making a sandwich." Morwenna explains as Athena strides in with the used cafetieres.

"OK." she says breezily to her daughter. "There should

be some cheese in there, I know we've run out of almost everything in the flat. My mind just hasn't been on it!" she acknowledges.

Morwenna's fair hair obscures her face as she, in her blue print dress and leggings, spreads butter on slices of Athena's home-made bread which she has placed directly on the counter, and adds slices of cheese and tomato. Licking the butter off her fingers, she turns to her mother.

"That man in there." she says pointing the knife in the direction of the sitting room.

"I saw him with your guest, the teacher one. I saw them in my shop the other day."

"Which man?" Priya asks, the room had been rather full.

"The tall Asian one, with the hat."

"When did you see them?" Rita is excited. Confirmation that Marina and Ash are together!

"At the weekend I think." Morwenna waves the knife in the air like a conductor's baton as she speaks, "They were looking at the clothes. Holding hands, that sort of thing." she adds vaguely.

"Looking happy together?" Rita ventures.

"Oh yes, I think so." Morwenna addresses the room as she exits, sandwich in hand, leaving behind the knife, the crumbs and the butter stains.

Chapter

5

"These violent delights have violent ends."

Friar Laurence in
Romeo and Juliet
by Shakespeare

Friday 26th July 2013

"Hurry up, Rita, we'll miss the train!" Priya is on her mobile, ringing her friend from Leicester station where she has been ready to catch the York train for 15 minutes, anxiously expecting the arrival of Rita and her brother.

"Nearly there." Rita replies optimistically although the station is still a quarter of a mile of busy traffic away. (Mohal always leaves things until the last minute! She thinks).

"We'll make it." her brother says confidently as he overtakes a car at the traffic lights and gets hooted at for his efforts.

The girls have a day off from Sundial. Athena is cool with this Rita tells her mother, Padma, as there is only one guest (Marina, the student teacher). Professor Rees ("Call me Angela.") had checked out, her studies done, but not before Rita could button hole her about her personal statement.

"Write from your heart." was her advice "I can see you are keen on history, put that passion across. Faculties want people who want to study their subject. It's that simple." Rita nodded at this, not convinced.

"Where are you applying to?" the Professor had asked. Rita was embarrassed to admit she had no Welsh Universities in her list, but Professor Rees did not seem to mind this. She approved of Oxford, of course, and thought Somerville

College a good choice. Rita said she was thinking of Exeter, Durham and York and that she would be visiting York soon to see what it was like.

"Oh you'll like it I'm sure," Professor Rees had smiled, "It's where I did my first degree so I'm biased. Have you considered Warwick? They have a good History Department". Rita had thanked her for the tip.

If Rita arrives in time, she Mohal and Priya are going to be shown round the campus at York by one of Mohal's friends. Breathlessly, having parked the car and run through the cavernous station entrance, the siblings practically collide with Priya before they all hasten through the barrier and clatter down the steps to throw themselves on the Derby train – just in time! They will change at Derby for York.

The girls have visited various University towns in order to produce their short list for Mr Thatcher's perusal. Although he has no power of veto, his advice is valued, especially as the girls have limited experience of the various Universities they might attend. "Campus or town. Near home or far. Content of course." The girls have mimicked Mr Thatcher's three golden rules for choosing a place to study. "And not the night life!" he always adds.

Rita and Priya are making a collection of sweat shirts from Universities to record their search. As Rita wants to read history and Priya to read medicine they realise the odds on them studying at the same place are long, but they know each other so well they are happy to give advice freely as to whether one or the other is likely to be happy in a particular place. Currently, Priya favours London, maybe University College, although her family are doubtful as to the safety or suitability of studying in the capital and would prefer her to choose a provincial university and one closer to home ("What's wrong with Birmingham? Or if you studied at Leicester you could stay at home." her mother hints). Rita is attracted by the idea of studying in a City with a lot of history, hence her interest in seeing what York has to offer. Now she must add Warwick to her list of potentials after her discussion with Professor Rees.

As the three sit alongside one another for the 20 minute part of the journey to Derby, Rita recalls that visiting Mohal at Hertfordshire University in April had helped her to realise that a new university was not for her; it was on a modern campus with some buildings less than five years old and others still under construction. The new law faculty was very impressive she had to admit, as was the auditorium and the library, and she could see why Mohal liked it – the sports facilities were very good with an Olympic size swimming pool and excellent gym facilities (Arsenal train here sometimes, Mohal told her proudly, and the Saracens rugby team).

The University, she learned, had expanded rapidly in the last 10 years and the new buildings were made possible by the closure of the aerospace business which used to occupy the site.

"The first jet was made here." Nayan was pleased to inform her in the family car as Jahi their father drove them to Mohal's house, "The de Havilland, that's why the main University building bears that name."

"Oh" said Rita, noticing other related street names – Mosquito Way and Runway Road.

"So what happened to the planes?" she asked.

"The work went elsewhere I guess." said Jahi as they passed a large building which had clearly been an aircraft hangar and was now a sports centre.

"Times change." thought Rita.

There were new industries on the rest of the old airfield site, as well as housing. The businesses were mostly related to distribution or telecommunications. Vans and lorries scuttled in and out of the business estate like worker ants and at certain times, when shifts changed, so did people, scurrying to catch their buses or rushing to and from car parks, all to serve the giant buildings which loomed, larger than the old aircraft hangar, over the carefully maintained roads and grassed areas (no ball games).

"The workers are mostly students or Eastern European," Mohal explained. "Those places tend to run on zero hours contracts so no one has any security and no one stays long. A friend of mine had only worked at one of those warehouses for a month when he became a supervisor because he had been there the longest!"

There were houses on part of the site, the sort of houses that look like they came from a childrens' story book – toy town style construction with mock Georgian windows and red tiled roofs. ("I bet there's not enough storage in them," Padma said, peering in as they drove by. "The houses look too thin." she added.)

Mohal's student house was one of these, in a crescent of identical dolls houses joined together. It looked like a stage set from the outside Rita thought. Inside there were 5 bedrooms and a large shared sitting room and kitchen area. Five boys shared the house and, although it was the beginning of term, when they visited the place was far from tidy.

All the surfaces (floor, tables, kitchen) were wipe-clean so Padma had set about that task while Mohal took Rita to ASDA to buy bin bags and Nayan helped Jahi find the garden under the rubbish which had accumulated ("Don't you put your rubbish out?" Padma asked her son. "We never know what day to do it." he replied. "You'd think the internet had never been invented," said Jahi, clicking onto the council website and printing out the information for his son).

"You'll never get any of your deposit back." Padma bemoaned (meaning the deposit to which she and Jahi had contributed Mohal's share).

"Oh no one bothers about that." said her son airily. Rita left the room before her parents exploded.

Mohal took them to St Albans in the afternoon. Having

seen how rundown the centre of Hatfield around ASDA was, with an accumulation of charity and loan shops, Rita thought St Albans was a much prettier town, with historic houses and buildings leading to a park with a lake which had swans and ducks, but no rowing boats, and some Roman ruins; much more to Rita's taste. They looked round the Abbey; Rita explained it was dissolved in 1539 and that much of its wealth had by then been squandered by Cardinal Wolsey, her pet project as the family knew, who made himself Abbot in 1521. He stripped the Treasury to pay towards his building of Cardinal College in Oxford. Part of the Abbey was now a school she noticed. It was clear from the tapestry in the Abbey which depicted the building of it that it was once a very powerful place, in fact, she knew, one of the richest in England at one time. It was even the venue, she found, for early discussions for Magna Carta.

Abbeys like this would have ruled everyday life for people from miles around, Rita thought. When the Abbey was dissolved the economy of the town would have been severely affected as the streams of visitors and pilgrims ceased and with it their demands for food and lodging. It would be like closing the Temples in India today, Rita thinks, recalling the traders and goods on offer at the entrances, the numbers of people visiting there, even her own purchases of flowers and candles when she visited the new Temple in Leicester. At the heart of the Abbey they found the restored shrine to St Alban, the Roman soldier and martyr who died protecting a Christian slave. Before dissolution the shrine to St Alban, and to Amphibalus, the slave he protected, would have attracted pilgrims from quite a distance and been helpful in promoting businesses in the area thought Rita, as well as encouraging a souvenir trade. You didn't have to believe in the power of relics to see their business potential.

Rita made them take the back road from St Albans, via Colney Heath, on their return to Mohal's house, so that the

journey took them past Tyttenhanger. She wanted to see the
site of the house in which Cardinal Wolsey, when he was at
the height of his powers, had entertained Henry VIII and
Katherine of Aragon for two weeks. They had stayed there to
avoid the 'sweating sickness' which was prevalent in London
at the time. The original palace had been surrounded by a
deer park and belonged to St Albans Abbey. Nothing of that
building remained, Rita knew. The current house on the site
(now used as offices) had a chapel at the top which, like the
church in north-west Leicestershire, at Staunton Harold, had
the rare distinction of having been built in the 1650s, during
the period known as the Commonwealth when the country
was ruled by Oliver Cromwell. Although created when the
Puritan religion held sway, the construction looked forward
to the restoration of the royal family and a higher form of
Anglicanism. This was fitting, perhaps, Rita thought, in view
of the religious changes and confusion which occurred in
the years after Wolsey's death. People must have got used to
hedging their bets on what form of Christian faith to follow,
Rita thought.

"Cardinal Wolsey," Rita says when the three of them have
changed trains at Derby and found their booked seats on the
train to York. These are at a table, which means she can open
her iPad easily to check her notes. Mohal groans and sinks
into his seat, rummaging in his pocket for his earphones so
he can tune out the history lesson. Priya shakes her head,
what now?

"He was Archbishop of York, even after he lost Henry's
favour. He went north to live in Yorkshire, at Cawood." ('You
told me this,' thinks Priya, 'Yorkshire, where Brian was from'.)
"Look!" says Rita excitedly, pointing to a picture of Cawood
Castle, "You can stay at the castle gatehouse!" She reads on
"Thomas Wolsey only came to Cawood when he had fallen
from power. It was here that he was arrested by the Earl of
Northumberland and turned back south where he died soon

after." Priya looks at the picture to humour her friend.

From the windows of the train as it journeys north through Derbyshire and Yorkshire they see the rural landscape interspersed with industrial buildings and towns. They pass several power stations, their strong round cooling towers reminiscent of the bold architecture of the Norman period except that these edifices were made for practical reasons, not for defence or to intimidate. Rita knows that some power stations are being dismantled as the reliance on domestic coal has changed since the miners' strike in the 1980s. Brian had told her that there were now only three deep mines left – Hatfield and Kellingley in Yorkshire and Thoresby in Nottinghamshire. The canals and branch railway lines, the coal preparation and coke plants, these had all lost their purpose and were as redundant as the workers who had once serviced them. If the buildings were not demolished they would eventually stand as hollow ruins across the landscape, like so many of the old Abbeys do she thinks.

Rita's phone rings. "It's Athena." Rita says to Priya as she presses the phone to answer the call.

"Sorry to bother you" their boss says to her, "I'm afraid the police have been on to me with some news."

"Oh?" Rita's interest is clear as her voice rises.

"Apparently they have the initial toxicology report on Brian. It turns out he had way too much insulin in his body. And as he was not diabetic or anything they're now treating it as a suspicious death."

"Oh dear" Rita manages, mouthing "Suspicious!" to Priya who is non-plussed and lifts her hands as if to ask a question. Rita waves a hand at her, meaning 'let me concentrate on what Athena is saying'.

The voice in her ear says, "So they are coming over to look at his things, Just wanted to check – you did put everything in the boxes?"

"Oh yes" Rita confirms, glad that this is the truth.

"Good, that's what I thought" says Athena.

"Well, see you tomorrow. Have a good day! And thanks Rita." she signs off.

"Well!" Rita is excited now. She brings Priya up to speed and Mohal too - he took out his earphones when he saw his sister talking animatedly.

"Too much insulin?" he says "How do you get that?"

Priya, the only one of them studying sciences, replies "Insulin is a natural hormone secreted by the pancreas. If a person is diabetic they don't secrete enough so they take insulin or a substance with similar effect – depends how they are with it."

"I thought only fat people got diabetes." says Mohal.

"Oh no" Priya explains "It can affect anyone but there are two types. Type one occurs because…"

"But Brian wasn't diabetic" Rita interrupts, "so how would he have too much insulin?"

"The likeliest explanation is an injection", says Priya.

"You mean suicide?" asks Mohal.

"Well presumably not," says Rita flatly "I think even the police would have thought it suspicious if Brian was found with a syringe and a bottle of insulin lying around in the boat."

"So someone else" says Priya.

"Uhuh." Rita agrees. "Now I wonder who would want to do that?"

* * *

When they arrive at York and step out of the station they are amazed at the sight of the Minster dominating in the distance and the yellow stone City walls snaking their way towards it. The Minster rising into the sky reminds Rita of the Abbey at St Albans and the Cathedral at Peterborough, all bold statements of faith and power, she thinks, and built by ordinary people who were living themselves in little more than hovels.

Cardinal Wolsey would have recognised the streets of York, if not their contents, and the Minster which was there when he was around, thinks Rita, as Mohal's friend, Jas, takes them on a quick tour. York is a labyrinth of meandering streets which make it difficult for Rita to find her bearings. There are several bridges which cross the river Ouse. This is a dominant feature of the town. Jas tells them that because it floods so frequently some pubs by the riverside have special entrances and exits so customers can still access them. They glimpse various old buildings which Rita would like to have time to explore – the Merchant Adventurer's Hall, Barley Hall, and the Treasurer's House to name some. There are fifty five steps up to Clifford's Tower, Jas tells her; this sits high above one quarter of the City and had been there since Norman times.

The University is outside the City. They take a bus to the campus, which Priya thinks is pretty, and set round a lake. It was built in the 1970s and with a lot of wooden framed doors and windows, so the effect is like an old fashioned holiday camp, Rita thinks. Jas explains the University has colleges for administrative purposes and that this helps with developing a social life too; most of his friends are in his college. As they drink fruit juice in the bar, looking out over the lake, it seems very tranquil for a busy University. Jas says it has a reputation for being hard working but there are plenty of activities too, as evidenced by the students in the corner discussing a forthcoming charity fashion show and the posters for plays and concerts across the campus.

On the train back, Rita recounts how there were many Abbeys in Yorkshire which got suppressed in the era after Wolsey. Rievaulx Abbey, a Cistercian monastery, was one of the richest; it was dissolved in 1538. Fountains Abbey ("The one they visited in The History Boys?" asks Priya, Rita nods) was founded by Benedictine monks and closed in 1539.

So what's the difference between the different types of monastery? Priya asks.

Rita looks up some information on the internet as their train moves southwards.

"Monasticism came from Egypt." she recites "You remember, we talked about the desert fathers in general studies?"

"Mmmn" Priya is not sure but surprisingly Mohal chips in, "Those crazy men on poles." before he puts his earphones on (So he was paying attention in some lessons, Rita thinks.)

"Some followed the rules of St Benedict – he was linked to a monastery in Italy called Monte Cassino, others followed St Francis, where poverty was a big theme - they tended to live among the people rather than in monasteries, and others followed St Augustine." she tells her friend, adding "There were several monasteries in the City of York and these were closed, including one in Fishergate. I love those old street names, don't you?"

So much change in so short a time, thinks Rita. The people must have thought the world was being turned upside down.

Chapter

6

"What an unkind hour is guilty of this lamentable chance."

Friar Laurence in
Romeo and Juliet
by Shakespeare

Saturday 27th July 2013

Athena is in a state of agitation, which is unusual for her. "What can be wrong?" Rita thinks when they arrive at Sundial. As it is Saturday they do not need to get there until 10am.

"Oh dear, I'm glad to see you girls," Athena says. "I don't know how we're going to manage. The police want to come and take away Brian's things today, then an inspector wants to interview us and Marina, the guest who was staying when Brian was- when he- oh dear… and Brian's wife - first wife - is coming to stay with his son and his mother. I don't know what I'm going to do with them all!"

"When is Edward coming back?" Priya asks a practical question. It is clear that Athena could do with some moral support. "Tomorrow, thank goodness!" Athena replies.

"And Morwenna?" Rita asks.

"In Ibiza with her friends, she'll be back next week." is the answer.

Rita and Priya set about their cleaning tasks, keeping their iPod volume turned down so they can hear the doorbell when the police arrive. Two uniformed women eventually ring the bell – their uniforms are more like track suits and Rita whispers "PCSOs" to Priya as they look at them over the bannister from the first floor. The policewomen decline tea, check that Rita and Priya packed up everything of Brian's from his room and leave saying "We may want statements from you all at some point."

('They didn't even take our fingerprints to eliminate us!' thinks Rita, who had been looking forward to that process.)

Sitting round the pine table for their break, Athena, Rita and Priya discuss how the rooms should be allocated to Brian's family.

"We can't put any of them in Daffodil – where Brian stayed - it just wouldn't be right." Athena asserts.

"How nimble is his mother? Can she manage stairs or use the stair lift? Would she be better in the ground floor room and the others upstairs?" this from Rita.

They agree that's the best solution. Brian's mother in Tulip on the ground floor, his ex-wife and son in Rose and Daisy on the top floor. Marina stays in Poppy on the first floor, which is the smallest and cheapest ("Not that I'm charging any of the family of course," Athena explains. "It wouldn't be right in the tragic circumstances." Rita wonders what Edward will make of that when he hears).

The girls are to stay to help the guests settle in when they arrive. "And you spoke to Brian, you knew him, so they'll probably be glad to talk to you about him." Athena tells them.

They muddle quietly through minestrone soup for lunch, keeping an eye on the local news on the television. Bad weather is forecast – there is the possibility of heavy rain later. Rita has noticed that the sky, and the atmosphere, had been getting darker; she had put it down to the general gloom which is settling over Sundial like a shroud. Presumably the play will have to be cancelled tonight if the forecast is right? The information that Brian's death is now regarded as suspicious has started to filter through to the Midlands news programme, but the national coverage does not mention it.

At just after three the bell goes, and Rita opens the door

to a substantial lady with white hair in a halo over her head, sensible shoes and a dark blue dress. She wears her handbag over her arm like Rita has seen in pictures of the woman prime minister, Mrs Thatcher, and her three quarter sleeves reveal aged wrinkled skin on her arms dotted with age spots.

"Are we in the right place?" the woman asks looking directly at Rita with piercing eyes. The same eyes Rita remembers with which Brian had looked at her.

She refrains from framing a sarcastic reply ('that depends where you want to be!') and opts instead for-

"Mrs Jackson?" and "Come in." Rita ushers her into the hall with all the care and dignity she would afford the Queen if she were to arrive on Sundial's doorstep. Mrs Jackson seems very mobile for her years and strides across the tiled floor to meet Athena and Priya. She is soon followed by a more tragic-looking pair. A round-faced overweight woman in her fifties enters with a holdall in each hand, followed by a tall young man in his late teens, wearing an Arran jumper and maroon corduroy trousers. ('He must be hot in that lot.' thinks Rita.) He has a lap top bag round his neck. Looking at the two of them struggling across the hall Rita thinks maybe they should reallocate the bedrooms and give the mother and son the room on the ground floor.

While introductions are being made, the bell rings again. 'Who can it be this time?' Rita thinks as she opens the door to a well-dressed, well-coiffed, woman in a black jersey Hobbs dress and black patent shoes.

"Hello, Rita," the woman says. Rita registers recognition. This is Jan, Brian's wife – ex-wife, second wife. She stayed at Sundial when Brian was here in May. She was one of those who had watched the croquet match from the terrace, gin and tonic in hand.

"I thought I should pop in." she says "I heard Brian's mother was staying here?"

'This should be interesting' Rita thinks as she closes the

door and Jan taps across the floor in her high heels.

* * *

Gathered round the distressed pine table half an hour later are Brian's mother, sitting ram rod straight on one side of the square, his first wife, Cynthia, with her elbows resting on the table, and their son Simon, who is absorbed in a game on his lap top, are together on the next side of the table. Across on the opposite side of the table sit Jan, who has placed her black jacket over the back of her chair, and Athena, who is positioned nearest the kitchen for catering purposes. Rita and Priya make up the fourth side of the table. The atmosphere is tense as the sky darkens ready for rain outside; it looks like a heavy downpour is imminent.

Priya and Rita pour tea and encourage everyone to partake of the freshly baked scones which Athena has laid on, together with substantial quantities of jam and cream. Cynthia helps herself keenly and starts to produce a red and white mixture on the top of the scone she has dissected. Margaret, Brian's mother, declines as she has diabetes. Jan empathises,

"Quite right Margaret. You have to be careful."

Jan, Rita recalls, manages a small nursing home in Nottingham so is presumably used to dealing with the elderly, not to mention her all-too evident desire to keep on the right side of Margaret. She seems to be playing a sort of 'ex daughter in law top trumps', first round having gone to Cynthia for bringing Margaret down from Grimethorpe.

"I don't know why we had to come." had been Margaret's conversational opener.

"The Leicester police wanted to speak to us." Cynthia explains, "It seemed the easiest way. And somehow it makes me feel closer to Brian."

Jan shoots her a hard look. "Why do you want to do that?

You've been divorced from him for donkey's years."

Jan is sipping Lapsang Souchong tea and nibbling at a piece of Athena's shortbread which she holds delicately between her manicured fingers.

"He grew out o' me and he grew out o' Grimethorpe" Cynthia says; Jan has clearly heard this before as she mimes the last part of Cynthia's sentence, mockingly tipping her head from side to side.

Simon, engrossed in his computer game in the corner, where Cynthia has poured him a glass of milk, says, "Dad gone. Dad gone. Dad not comeback, like Roger."

"Roger?" says Athena, alarmed. Simon does not look up. He does not realise he is being asked a question.

"Tell Athena who Roger was." says Cynthia.

"My rabbit." says Simon, still without turning his attention from the screen. Cynthia smiles and shrugs an apology towards Athena. "You'll have to forgive him. He doesn't mean to be rude."

"Don't worry." says Athena, thinking how trying it must be to parent a child with learning difficulties, and to help them to navigate their way into the adult world.

"We didn't lose touch." Cynthia is saying through pursed lips. "Brian took an interest in Simon. We were talking about his future – Simon's that is. He finishes school next year and we – I – want him to go away to College if he can. I know Brian wanted him to have the best we could afford." ("He could afford, you mean" Jan utters under her breath.) "I don't know how things are now, financially." Cynthia finishes quietly and awkwardly, looking in Jan's direction.

Suddenly Rita is aware of what has brought these three very different women together. As well as being united in grief for Brian, each of them was financially tied to him too. He owned the house he shared with his mother, his first wife wanted money for their disabled son. And Jan? What was the basis of their divorce settlement? The one they had been discussing that May bank holiday when Rita had seen her last?

* * *

Sunday 26th May 2013

It was unusual for Sundial to be busy on a Sunday, but the late May bank holiday weekend was exceptional. Rita and Priya were asked to help with a diamond wedding anniversary lunch for Athena's neighbours, Alf and Daphne Flowers, who live in a ground floor flat two doors down from Sundial. They had been supporters of the Bed and Breakfast ever since Athena and Edward had opened it 5 years ago. They encouraged their family to stay there when they visited and the place became a home from home for family gatherings, saving Daphne and Alf the effort of catering and clearing up.

Sundial worked perfectly for the younger great grandchildren who could have the run of the back garden, which was enclosed and safe for them to roam in; the older children played the games in the sitting room and there was space for everyone to gather in groups to talk and to enjoy a buffet lunch arranged artistically by Athena.

On this day, a congratulatory cake stood in the middle of the table, together with the card they had received from Buckingham Palace, surrounded by the vegetarian buffet platters Athena had put together. The table groaned at the edges with cheeses and fruit and there was homemade trifle for those with a sweet tooth. Rita and Priya were kept busy running between the kitchen, the dining room and the sitting room, making sure the guests' plates and glasses were recharged with food and non-alcoholic beverages. This was made more of a challenge by the young children running in and out – potential hazards were not perceived until the last minute and several disasters were only just averted. The parents of these whirling dervishes seemed blissfully unaware of the potential chaos, not attempting to stop their offspring from experimenting with the stair lift until Athena put her foot down (unusual for her), truly making themselves 'at home' and only calling aimlessly and occasionally "Lucinda, where are you?" or "Oliver, what are you doing?"

Into this hectic scene, Rita recalled, had entered Brian Jackson, looking sheepish and as if he wished he had a cloak of invisibility, and Jan, his soon-to-be-ex-wife, who did not look out of place at the party at all; in fact she looked as if the party was in her honour, in her designer dress ("Was it Victoria Beckham or Mary Portas?", Priya wondered, her sister Meera would know), large sunglasses ('Was the light really so bright?' thought Rita) and nude high heels ('How does she walk in those?' Rita wanted to know).

While Brian looked embarrassed to be intervening in the festivities, Jan succeeded in looking disdainful and as if the party was interrupting her, not the other way round.

"Sorry to arrive now." Brian had apologised to Athena. "I need to be at the theatre for 3." he pushed his maroon jacket sleeves, worn over a blue shirt and with beige chinos, along his arms as he spoke, "OK if I just pop my things upstairs? Daffodil as usual?"

Athena had nodded, "Thanks Brian, that's great." Then "And you must be Mrs…" she had hesitated.

"Jan Jackson, yes." the confident looking woman had said, adjusting the large bag resting on her designer shoulder pad.

"I've put you in Bluebell, next to Brian." (So they were not in the same room Rita noticed.) "I hope you can manage. The party will be over by 4."

She indicated the stairs in an effort to usher the new arrivals away. Rita lost track of Jan and Brian after that. She assumed they escaped in the melee of the party. Neither was present when she, Athena and Priya were working their way through the piles of used crockery and cutlery and hoovering up the cake crumbs which were all that remained from the harmonious atmosphere and gracious gratitude of the Flowers family gathering.

"I'm glad we don't do this every day." Athena said as the three of them sank on to the sofas – Rita and Priya on the battered leather one, Athena stretching full length on the golden chintz, two of the cushions (LAUGH and LOVE) under her head.

"You girls did well. You'll sleep well tonight!" she added just as a noise could be heard outside the front door – they had heard a car arrive moments earlier. A key turned in the lock and an agitated Brian entered followed by an animated Jan.

"Can't we discuss this reasonably?" Brian was saying.

"I am being reasonable" this from Jan whose designer handbag was now in her hand, like a weapon she might throw at any time, "William and I need your financial support; we won't manage without it." she added.

Both paused when they got into the hall and realised they had an audience, the sitting room door being open. Athena waved a hand at them over the back of the sofa she was lying on, Rita and Priya crouched lower on their sofa in discomfort. Jan cleared her throat, turned on her heel and strode quickly upstairs.

Recalling this argument, Rita wonders whether to mention it when the police inspector calls.

Chapter

7

"The grey eyed morn smiles on the frowning night."
Friar Laurence in
Romeo and Juliet
by Shakespeare.

Sunday July 28th 2013

The Inspector has arranged to talk to them all early on Sunday afternoon ("Why Sunday?" says Edward when Athena tells him this on the telephone He was hoping for a lift from the airport but will have to make his own way now.) When she opens the door to the Inspector, at first Rita confuses him with one of the theatre company until he produces his warrant card which discloses his name to be Jamie Bridge. He is boyish- looking with ginger hair tumbling into his eyes ("Don't they have to get a haircut these days?" says Padma, Rita's mother, when she sees him later). He is casually dressed in jeans and t-shirt and wears flip flops on his feet ('How will he chase burglars?' Rita thinks).

He speaks to Athena when she comes to greet him in the hall, her auburn hair escaping from a blue scarf tied casually on her head.

"That was quite a storm last night!" Athena says as she shows him into the dining room, the girls following. "I gather there's a lot of clearing up to be done?"

"Yeah," he agrees, "Flash floods in Market Harborough I gather, lots of water to be cleared out. Overtime for the traffic guys." he adds.

He sits at the table and opens a note book but makes no attempt to write anything down. ('Not exactly Inspector

Gadget,' thinks Rita, 'hasn't he heard of electronic communications?')

"Now then." he looks around. Then, showing he is a creature of the 21st century after all, "CCTV?"

When Athena tells him there is none the Inspector exhales deeply. "Really?" an incredulous tone escapes from his lips.

"I work on trust," explains Athena, spreading out her hands which are red from having recently been dipped in washing up water; today she wears a long turquoise top over blue leggings and sandals and manages to look as if she might be off to the beach any minute. "I don't want to spy on people." she adds.

"Ok" Jamie Bridge says reluctantly, closing his pad and raising his eyebrows. 'This is obviously going to be more difficult than he anticipated', Rita thinks.

"Well, there's CCTV on the main road. That may tell us something." he adds with more conviction.

"When did each of you last see Brian Jackson?" he next asks. By now they are seated like an interview panel, the three women on one side of the pine table, Jamie Bridge on the opposite side. He sits casually, with his long legs stretched out under the table and his note pad, closed, in front of him.

Between them they explain how Brian rose late on Monday morning, having got in the previous evening at about 10pm (there is no performance of the play on a Sunday, they explain, so Sunday was his one night off). They describe him pottering about making his own toast that morning while Athena tidied the kitchen. They explain how he gave Rita and Priya permission to clean his room ("don't tidy anything away!" he had joked). None of them had seen him leave the house later, but Athena confirmed he was gone when she returned from the supermarket at about 1.30.

"And what frame of mind would you say he was in?" ('What frame of mind is anyone in?' Rita thinks).

"He seemed fine to me." Athena takes the lead.

"Yes." says Rita. Priya nods.

Rita adds, "He was joking with us, teasing us. So he seemed in a good mood."

"You didn't see him later on Monday, or early on Tuesday? After the Monday performance for example?" Inspector Bridge asks them all. Rita and Priya shake their heads.

Athena says, "I saw him come back to Sundial. I'm not sure of the time. About 11pm? I saw him from the window of my flat. I can just see the feet of the guests as they go up the steps to the front door of Sundial. There were two people, a man and a woman, I think, on the steps, and the man was Brian - I saw his desert boots. I had been meditating so I wasn't quite with it." Athena produces one of her Buddhist quotes, "We are shaped by our thoughts; we become what we think. When the mind is pure, joy follows like a shadow that never leaves."

Jamie Bridge is taken by surprise. After a pause, the Inspector coughs "Who else was staying here on Monday and Tuesday?" is his next question.

"Marina Hutchinson. She is on a course at the University connected with Teach First. You know, the fast track teaching course for graduates." Athena explains.

"Hmmn" the Inspector notes this information down assiduously, as if teaching is a career option he may consider for himself.

"Marina should be here soon." Athena adds, looking at the clock in the dining room. "We thought you'd want to kill as many birds as possible with one visit." she goes on, regretting the metaphor as soon as it is uttered.

"Very thoughtful." says Jamie Bridge distractedly. Then "You cleared his room and put everything in the boxes which the boys in blue took away yesterday?"

Rita and Priya nod, both judging it wise not to point out that the boxes were taken by women 'in blue' not men.

"You didn't keep anything? Find anything afterwards?" he

adds encouragingly. The girls shake their heads.

"OK" says Jamie Bridge, "It's just that his mobile is missing. Know anything about that?" He looks at the girls directly and suddenly intimidatingly.

"No we don't." says Rita clearly "It wasn't in his room." says Priya.

Athena adds "He would have had it with him, surely?"

Inspector Bridge has no reaction to this.

"OK." he says in a decisive tone.

Then "Do you do laundry for guests?" It's an unexpected question, to Athena.

"Well, no," she says "I only have a washing machine in my flat – for family use. I send the bedding and towels to the cleaners." she adds for clarity.

"And there were no shirts in the wardrobe or drawers?" Jamie Bridge turns to Rita and Priya.

Who look at each and think for a moment – "Well no." they say together.

"Mmmn." is the Inspector's response as he notes that down too.

(Rita wonders what the Inspector's notes must look like. Will he type them up afterwards? She also wonders if Jamie Bridge has spoken to Aaran, because now she comes to think of it, he said Brian was wearing a shirt after the performance, yet when he was found he was in jogging clothes, and there was no shirt in the room. Does this explain the question? Where could the shirt have gone?).

"Has Brian's car turned up?" Rita decides to ask a question.

"As a matter of fact it has." confirms the Inspector. "It was near the entrance to the Park, close to the boating lake, actually."

"Now if I could see Mr Jackson's room. I take it no one has used it since he…" he pauses, "left?"

Athena confirms this and shows Inspector Bridge up to Daffodil.

"Well," says Rita with an air of curiosity when he has left the dining room, "Brian wouldn't usually park by the boating lake, that's asking for a ticket. He told me he liked to park down one of the side streets."

"So he moved his car?" says Priya, joining in her friend's train of investigative thought.

"Yeah, before climbing into a boat and overdosing on insulin without any syringe or other equipment." says Rita thoughtfully, then, "No, I think someone helped Brian leave this life."

At that moment the distinctive engine of Marina's VW beetle can be heard as it turns into the front drive at Sundial.

"And I think that someone used Brian's car to do so. We should visit the park this afternoon." Rita finishes as she rises to answer the anticipated doorbell.

Priya rolls her eyes and studies one of the magazines on the table. Really Rita is impossible! But she knows her friend is implacable once her interest is aroused.

Marina has a large bag slung over her shoulder as she enters the hall, and outsized sunglasses obscure most of her face. Wearing her trademark white cardigan, she sits at the dining table when Inspector Bridge returns from his consideration of Daffodil and anything it may offer by way of clues as to Brian's last hours.

Rita has made Marina a cup of tea for her interrogation (if the languid approach adopted by Inspector Bridge can be given that description). ('Like being mauled by a dead sheep didn't someone say once?' Rita thinks.)

Marina is awkward and hesitant, never having come into contact with the police before. Her decision to do Teach First had been reached after various attempts at other careers she explains to Inspector Bridge who is writing furiously now- working at a cosmetic clinic and at a telephone marketing company among them- and she adds that her parents are afraid that this business with Brian will deter her from going through with the University course.

Coughing nervously, Marina says she went to bed about midnight on Monday, using the Wi-Fi to catch up on her email before she put on a Mad Men DVD, she has a box set. She thought she heard voices about 1 o'clock, then she must have fallen asleep. She may have heard someone say, about 2 or 2.30 she can't be sure, "Good night then Brian." when she got up to go to the bathroom and before she dozed off again.

"Did you hear anything else?" Jamie Bridge leans towards Marina as he speaks.

"Well... I might have heard a noise – I was asleep so I can't be sure whether the noise was inside the house or outside - it was a mechanical noise, like a washing machine, that was a bit later - I can't be sure when." Marina has a tissue in her hand which she is stretching out and screwing up alternately. ('A washing machine?' thinks Rita, 'Does that explain the laundry question?')

Inspector Bridge takes Marina back to Monday morning. Had she seen Brian then? No. The only time they had spoken was on Sunday night. They passed on the stairs, Marina told him. She had breakfasted and left before Brian on Monday. Marina gives the Inspector her home address and leaves the dining room to go upstairs to her room on the first floor.

Cynthia, Margaret and Jan all parade in next, gathered by Athena from corners of the sitting room, the garden and its furniture being too wet from the previous night's rain to be enjoyable. Simon does not join them for the discussion. Rita can hear him talking to his computer in the sitting room ("He wouldn't understand." says Cynthia.). As Rita hovers with the tea pot, they give their home details and say that Brian was not unhappy so far as they know. He was not in any disputes that they are aware of. There was some enmity going back years among the mining community, Cynthia and Margaret explain, but that was mostly envy at his success says Margaret. Then the Inspector says sensitively-

"Mr Jackson's father passed away some time ago I believe?" to which Margaret gives a decisive nod.

"And there is no other family?" Jamie Bridge adds.

"There was Bill my brother, he died a few weeks back. He had a soft spot for Brian. Left him some money I believe." Margaret explains.

Rita can feel the other women in the room assenting to this, so they all knew about the inheritance she thinks.

"And no siblings?" Inspector Bridge asks next.

"I beg your pardon?" says Margaret abruptly as if she has not understood.

"Brian had no brothers or sisters?" he expands.

"Ian" Margaret astounds Rita by saying, "His brother's Ian but we never see him or talk to him. He went work in the Nottingham pits and that was that." She folds her arms as if to close the subject.

Rita thinks she needs to get back to the library to see what else she can find out about Ian Jackson. He had not featured in any of the interviews Brian had given at the height of his fame.

As the Inspector is leaving Sundial, taking with him the guests' registration forms for the last 6 months, Padma, Rita's mother, arrives, car keys in hand. Having spoken to Athena, she and the girls come down the steps of Sundial in the wake of Jamie Bridge. Rita notices that the Inspector drives a VW Golf, which is currently parked alongside Marina's beetle. She deftly steps into the back seat of Padma's car to sit alongside Priya who has climbed in the other side.

"I'll drop you at Abbey Park on the way to Jaina's". Rita's mother says. She is planning a long discussion with her sister, away from Rita's prying ears, about which Universities would be most suitable for Rita. "Mohal will take you home later Priya." Padma adds.

When they get to Abbey Park, Mohal is waiting. He walks up to them and gestures to the lake immediately." 'Hashtag funandgames' going on there." he says grinning. Rita looks across the grass to the water's edge. The lake, usually on a summer Sunday afternoon occupied by several boats, young people squealing and shouting, men showing off, women pretending to be alarmed, was today cordoned off by police tape ('So they are taking Brian's death seriously' Rita thinks.)

There is a police caravan parked by the lake, which Rita presumes they are using as a temporary base. As she scans the scene Rita sees a diver in a frog suit in the middle of the lake wave something in the air. Another diver comes to relieve them of the object. The water is shallow enough for them to be wading but every so often one of the divers goes beneath the surface and reappears. Rita wonders what they are hoping to find; maybe the insulin and syringe?

"Cool," she says, "Let's watch from the café." As they walk to the entrance they pass the statue of Cardinal Wolsey which Rita pauses to inspect. Priya, shy in the presence of Mohal, follows Rita into the café and selects a seat by the window so they can keep an eye on the search of the lake. The café is busy, with families vying for the attention of the assistants who are occupied talking with customers about the search.

"Don't know how long they'll be here."

"Don't think it's anything to worry about."

"Just being thorough."

"Things like that hardly ever happen in the Park."

"Oh look," says Priya as Mohal arrives at their table with mint tea and wafer biscuits (Rita's favourite). Priya has spotted the Inspector who spoke to them earlier, outside by the police tape.

"Inspector Bridge." says Rita, explaining to her brother. She notes that Jamie Bridge has swapped his flip flops for green wellingtons.

"At least they're doing something." is Mohal's reaction "I hope they're not accusing you of anything?" he half jokes. Mohal has a distrust of the police, having been stopped by them in his car several times for no apparent reason. ("As if black men can't drive cars!" he says in exasperation). He did get in with a group at University who were vehemently opposed to the police, but Rita thought he had been seeing less of them and hoped he was not going to take his frustration too far.

"They seem to think Brian's mobile phone is missing." Priya says quietly, not wanting people at the other tables to hear.

"I hope they didn't accuse you!" Mohal says indignantly.

"Let's talk about something else." says Rita quickly, turning to Priya, "Any more thoughts on whether you will apply to Oxford?" she asks her friend.

* * *

Rita and Priya had not known what to make of Oxford when they arrived there in April on a trip arranged by Mr Thatcher, head of university applications at their school. They had travelled with others from their year – six in all. A mini-bus had met them at the station at Oxford and they climbed aboard to greet 5 other pupils from various places – Wolverhampton, Bristol, and Hartlepool. The cheery guide – an undergraduate in Biological Sciences called Ben – had explained the itinerary as the minibus crawled through the midday traffic to Magdalen College. Apart from a few familiar shop fronts, which they glimpsed along the High Street, Oxford seemed like a town made up of high stone-walled buildings like churches. The ancient yellow façades with few windows which presented themselves to the roads they passed along were too tall to see over, they were like City walls designed to keep invaders out. The girls tried to peer in at gateways to see what was beyond, but were mostly thwarted by wooden doors or barriers.

Turning into Magdalen College, Rita realised that

Magdalen School was on the opposite side of the road. She recalled that Cardinal Wolsey, although supposed to be the son of a butcher, had been clever enough to attend both the school and the college and took his BA at the age of fifteen.

Once through the gates the girls realised that beyond the forbidding walls and narrow entrance lay a whole different world. There were beautiful buildings and well- tended grounds, accessible by those who were privileged to work or study there. The College square ('Or was it a quad?' Rita thought) had on one side the famous Church tower where, Rita knew, on May Day the choristers sang. ('So the bridge they had seen must be the one from which the students sometimes throw themselves recklessly on the same occasion,' Rita realised.)

They were ushered into a hall where they met other pupils, some displaying apparent confidence, others looking nervous, and were addressed on issues like how to make the best of your application,how to make the best of your college interview, and there were talks on the subjects for which Oxbridge required applicants to sit a special exam.

After a buffet lunch they were free to wander about the town and given a map so they could identify any colleges they passed, and find their way back to the station. Priya and Rita had found themselves looking over the bridge near the Botanical gardens, at the punts moored together waiting for the better weather and the tourists, then they walked along the High Street and turned left to walk past Merton College, arriving at Folly Bridge and the entrance to Christchurch, where they paid to go in.

Christchurch was very imposing, Rita thought, and quite in keeping with a Cardinal who thought he had 'made it'. Rita was excited to find the College's coat of arms were those of Wolsey, granted to him by the College of Arms in 1525. She realised that the College had been added to and altered since Wolsey's time, including a gate-tower designed by Sir Christopher Wren, but she found the layout, with the Great Quad, breath-taking in its size and ambition. To build his 'Cardinal College' Wolsey had taken money from several establishments including an Abbey called St Frideswide in Oxford and nearby Wallingford Priory, she told Priya. On his downfall the College was suppressed, but Henry VIII re-founded it as Christchurch, using money from the dissolution, renaming it, and making the partially demolished Priory Church the Cathedral for the recently created diocese of Oxford.

They found the nave of the Church part sumptuous and opulent with high ceilings rising up to the skies and beautifully glazed windows in bright colours and images. They were most impressed with the hall with its hammer beam roof, which was used as the dining hall of Hogwarts in the Harry Potter films, they knew. They stared upwards with awe, sharing their excitement with a predominantly Chinese group of tourists. The front of the building they found faced onto fields (Christchurch meadows) and the river. They learnt that Charles I had held his Parliament in the Great Hall during the Civil War and that a cannon ball from the Parliamentarian side had hit the wall of the hall.

Thirsty after absorbing all that history, they picked up a drink from the café opposite the College, then walked back up through the town to the station for their train.

* * *

After their tea, Rita, Priya and Mohal walk a little in Abbey Park and around the low walls which show where the Abbey buildings had been. The Abbey was built by Augustinian canons in honour of the Virgin Mary, Rita has read. It was endowed with the possessions of a college of canons known as the College of St Mary de Castro and no doubt Henry VIII benefitted when the Abbey surrendered itself for dissolution in 1538, although the corruption of various abbots meant that the Abbey's debts exceeded its no doubt substantial income by then. Everything started with the Catholic Church in this country, Rita thinks, recalling the colleges and buildings in Oxford. Once this place would have been a place of quiet devotion, she thinks, but it does not have a tranquil air today; this is partly because, as it is Sunday, the place is overrun with children and boisterous teenagers with energy to expend, and partly because each of the three of them is aware every time they hear a shout that it may be the police who have found something.

They buy an ice cream and sit on the grass to watch the activity in the lake, an event which has attracted other bystanders – 'rubber neckers' Mohal says, but it does not stop him from taking an interest. The police have a pile of finds by now, mostly old boots, shopping bags, a rusty bike and a shopping trolley. Nothing that suggests it is linked to whatever happened to Brian as far as Rita can see.

Suddenly, there is a more excited shout from one of the divers. They are holding something aloft. It is a small metal object. Rita is sure this looks like a mobile phone. But is it Brian's? And can it tell the police anything if it's been in the water for several days? She wonders.

Chapter

8

"Riddling confession finds but riddling shift."
Friar Laurence in
Romeo and Juliet
by Shakespeare

Monday July 29th 2013

A week after Brian's last performance, Rita and Priya travel with Padma and Nayan, Rita's younger brother, to Abbey Park. They are going to see the Dragon Company perform Romeo and Juliet thanks to free tickets which Caroline has provided.

"I hope it's not too sloppy." Nayan says in the car. "It's a bit of a girls' play, innit?" Nayan has started a growth spurt and like Alice in Wonderland after she ate the cake with 'Eat Me' written on it, his arms and legs seem to be growing at a rate which is alarming to him and concerning to his family. A body which used to fit neatly in the back of the car now sprawls and projects, like an unwieldy tree, and he is prone to bang his head or bump into objects which he was previously adept at avoiding. It is as if his personal sat-nav is failing. Rita and Priya have therefore allowed him the privilege of the front passenger seat and these provocative remarks he addresses to them by turning round in his seat to face them.

Rita flutters her eyes in exasperation but knows not to rise to the bait. Nayan is trying to provoke an argument.

"There will be fights as well." Priya offers, "Don't forget, Tybalt gets killed."

"And it's very sad." puts in Padma.

"It's a tragedy, after all." Rita adds.

It is a pleasant, balmy evening, the weather having been fine since the thunderstorms and flash floods of Saturday, like a child making up for its bad behaviour. Padma has brought cushions and rugs ("Just in case.") and they all have jumpers to protect them as the evening air cools. The audience is seated on temporary benches stacked in rows four high. They locate their seats on the second row. ('Not too near the fights!' Priya thinks.)

As the characters appear and the play unfolds, Rita finds herself looking at the actors, and Ash the assistant stage manager, who can scarcely be seen as he surreptitiously moves scenery, presses buttons and switches. 'That's why he wears black clothes all the time.' Rita thinks. She is not concentrating on the play, but wondering if any of the Company could have wished Brian harm? Rita is also remembering a conversation with Marina earlier that day, and wondering if the girl has yet done anything about it?

* * *

Rita had been on her own at Sundial that morning, Priya taking time off to work on her personal statement. After doing all the rooms which were occupied – only two that day - Rita had gathered up the rubbish bags – one with waste for recycling, the other with general waste - and taken them to the bins outside, carefully clutching them in one hand while she reached with the other for the heavy key which always hangs by the kitchen door to give access for disabled guests. As she was depositing the correct waste in each bin, she realised she was not alone in the garden. Sitting on a bench on the terrace, where Rita had felt Jan's eyes boring into the players during the croquet match in May, was Marina, puffing on an electronic cigarette.

"Hello." Rita greeted her, peeling off her yellow Marigolds which she thought were are not a good look.

"I didn't know you smoked." Rita added.

Marina looked down at the slim white cigarette substitute in her hand.

"I'm not supposed to." Marina admitted, grimacing, "and it's a bad habit to have if you want to teach kids." she shrugged, "But I need the nicotine sometimes!" she exclaimed "And who wouldn't if they were trapped in classrooms with noisy kids all day!" Her voice rose to a nervous crescendo.

"Oh dear," said Rita sympathetically. "Things not going well?" she invited.

"Oh it's not the teaching." Marina explained, taking another draw on the cigarette,

"It's relationships. It's life. You'll find out soon enough for yourself, if you haven't already." she added with a world weary sigh.

"Men?" Rita ventured "More trouble than they're worth?" Rita had heard this sentiment from the popular girls at school.

"Something like that." Marina sighed and untied her white cardigan from her waist, putting it round her shoulders like a shawl.

"Oh Rita, I don't know what to do for the best." she burst out.

Rita decided to sit on the bench beside the woman to find out what was wrong, recalling as she did so the strange scene she had witnessed from a distance between Marina and Ash, and what Morwenna had said about seeing them together in her shop.

"Is it Ash?" she ventured.

"You know?" Marina was surprised.

"Well I've seen you together, that's all." Rita admitted.

"Oh dear," Marina looked rueful. "Busted." She barked a laugh. "Maybe we should have come clean. I wanted to, but Ash said we shouldn't, it couldn't make any difference."

"Difference to what?" Rita was intrigued. ('What do

Marina and Ash know, what have they done?' she was thinking.)

"It's just that," Marina started to put her E cigarette away, "Oh dear," she looked at Rita sheepishly under her lashes, "You'll think badly of me." she pulled a rueful face.

"What is it?" Rita was keen to know.

"Well, that night, the Monday night, I didn't tell the police the full story."

"Oh dear." Rita said, trying not to sound judgmental.

"Well I don't think it matters," her companion said in a voice which betrayed her doubts.

"Do you think I should tell them?" Marina appealed to Rita, a girl whose lack of experience she had just lamented but whose opinion she now craved.

"Tell them what?" Rita is in the dark; what secret is Marina keeping?

"That Ash was here, on Monday night, he stayed in my room. I know we're not meant to have visitors overnight – and we were drinking – so I didn't want to say anything in front of Athena. And I couldn't see what difference it could make to what happened to Brian."

"OK." Rita spoke slowly, trying to absorb this new information. She had so many questions she wanted to ask. How did they meet? Have they been going out long?

"So when did Ash arrive?" is the question she plumps for. The background can come later.

"I picked him up from the Park after the performance and drove him back. We got in about 11. Athena was in her flat so she didn't see us."

"When did he leave?" Rita's next question.

"About 6 in the morning. He went to get the first bus back to his digs, then he wanted to get to the Park to sort out the electrics."

"And what you told the police about what you heard that night…?" Rita pressed.

"Is the truth." Marina said vehemently. "Except that it wasn't me that heard it. I'm a heavy sleeper. Ash said he heard someone say 'Goodnight Brian' and it was Ash who thought he heard a mechanical noise."

"Mmmmn." Rita mulled this over. That explained why Marina could not be more specific when questioned by Inspector Bridge. "And Brian was here when Ash went out?"

"Well that's the odd thing. No he wasn't. At least he wasn't in his room. Ash said the door was open and no sign of Brian. So Ash closed his door on his way past."

Rita thought, if Brian had gone for a run he had left very early then, before six, which was not his usual habit after a performance.

"I think this is important." she had said to the older girl. "You really should tell Inspector Bridge."

"Oh dear. What will people think of me?" Marina wailed.

"Better they know the truth." Rita said. "What Ash has to say about Brian not being in his room so early in the morning may be relevant. We don't know. How did you meet Ash anyway?" (Rita had been desperate to ask this.)

"I'm going to teach English and drama," Marina explained. She had been to a dress rehearsal of the play, met Ash back stage and things had developed from there.

"It's not a serious thing," she had said to Rita. "I expect it's a case of a girl in every town for him. But he doesn't want to get into trouble with Caroline for larking around when there's a play on. I gather she can be quite proprietorial with the Company members; and I didn't want Athena to know I had a visitor overnight… oh dear."

She stood up then. "Yes." Marina said, resolute now.

"I have to come clean. Thanks Rita. Oh dear."

As she had watched the figure of Marina retreating into Sundial, Rita was not sure if what Marina had said was the whole truth? What really happened and were she and Ash involved in some way? Is that the real reason they were having their whispered argument in the street?

* * *

While her friend's concentration wanders, Priya is intently watching the action on the temporary stage. Priya sympathises with Juliet when she grows alarmed at her parents' plan to marry her to Paris. It is one of Priya's fears that an unsuitable husband will be found for her. When Juliet says "Is there no pity sitting in the clouds that sees into the bottom of my grief? O sweet mother, cast me not away! Delay this marriage for a month, a week, or if you do not, make the bridal bed in that dim monument where Tybalt lies." Priya can feel tears forming at the back of her eyes.

Meanwhile, Rita's attention turns from Ash to the actors. Judith, who plays the nurse with great energy, is the only woman on stage who looks strong enough to kill a man, assuming some strength was required, which Rita assumes it was. How else could Brian have been overpowered, and insulin administered? The actresses, playing Juliet, her mother, and various courtiers, also appear as pages and soldiers to make up the numbers when the men are on stage. Their slight boyish figures lend themselves to this deception and, after all, in Shakespeare's time the roles would have been reversed and boys would have played women, Rita thinks.

What about Caroline, the stage manager? She is a strong personality, Rita has noticed, and she thought Caroline was flirting with Brian when she saw them larking around at the croquet match. Did he hurt her feelings? Was she offended, wounded by a rejection? Rita thinks, murder would be a bit of a drastic response, surely? But what if Caroline was jealous after all; Jan had been around in May and Marina had said that Caroline could be proprietorial with people in the Company.

What about the men? Ash found the body so that

automatically makes him a suspect, Rita knows from detective programmes – did he find him because he was the last to see him alive? Jacob is a diabetic so might have access to insulin – it depended on what treatment he was on - and Jacob now had the Friar Laurence part, but surely that was not a sufficient motive?

As they throw punches in the crowd scenes and thrust and parry with their swords to engineer Tybalt's death, all the men look strong, lithe and agile and capable of violence, Rita thinks; but of course, she checks herself, they are only acting, pretending, feigning. All this is rehearsed and planned. Poor Brian was not given a chance to rehearse.

The fight scene makes Rita recall what Judith had said, about a fight Brian got into when he was touring in Doncaster. What could have triggered feelings so strong that blows were struck, and who hit out first? She wonders, someone who had been a friend, or a relative? She recalls her researches in the Central Library, with Mohal's help, after she had finished at Sundial that day. Ian Jackson was Brian's older brother by 3 years she had discovered. Some material from the local papers recently depicted him in an article about the growing trend for tattoos, revealing a colourful tattoo on his chest and neck. The archive of the Nottingham papers showed he had been involved in a mines rescue operation in the mid-1990s at Thoresby colliery and questioned about a death at Ollerton colliery during the strike. The Thoresby story was from around the time that Brian's acting career was starting to take off; the article gave Ian's age and said he was married with a son. When she googled his name, a few articles came up suggesting that an Ian Jackson (impossible to tell if it was the same one) had appeared in amateur productions in the Nottingham area. So perhaps Brian was not the only actor in the family, Rita had thought.

During the interval Rita gets ice creams for all of them while Padma queues for the Ladies. The stage is above some of the Abbey walls, with the outline of trees darkening in the distance and the ruins of the manor house, which are also in the Park, looking sinister in the twilight shadows. The stage lights start to take effect as they resume their seats and the spotlights swallow up the gathering darkness around the stage area. Looking up, stars can been seen like tiny spot lights in the blue black sky.

The lake is some distance away, no longer cordoned off. 'But anyone – especially the actors, could get rid of evidence in it any time?' Rita thinks. As far as she knows, no one has been searched.

When the final curtain comes – there is no curtain but the players walk back on stage, all holding hands in a long line - the actors are shaking off their characters and becoming themselves, getting ready to change for home, like Brian did that one last time a week ago, Rita thinks. Did he come back to Sundial with someone - a woman - as Athena thought? If so, when did he leave? Why was he in his running gear so early in the morning? And why was he wearing his reading glasses as Ash had said? Where was his shirt and had the police found his phone? Most importantly, what was Inspector Bridge doing about any of this?

Chapter

9

"If aught in this miscarried by my fault, let my old life be sacrificed, some hour before the time, unto the rigour of severest law"

Friar Laurence in
Romeo and Juliet
by Shakespeare

Wednesday July 31st 2013

At 10am on Wednesday, Rita and Priya are hoovering in the sitting room at Sundial. There is more to tidy up today as they both had Tuesday off. Yesterday Rita had tried a few drafts of her personal statement and read some out loud to Priya when they skyped.

* * *

"History is my passion. I like to find out about characters from the past and what happened to them. For example I am currently researching Cardinal Wolsey."

"Not him again!" said Priya.

"Professor Rees said write from the heart." Rita countered, "And I am interested in him. Now where was I? Oh yes, 'Because he failed to please the King by obtaining the annulment he wanted, the truth about him may be obscured.' As Mark Twain said, 'the very ink with which history is written is merely fluid prejudice.' I have visited various sites associated with Wolsey to get a feel for his life and times."

"Have you?" Priya was flicking through a magazine looking at pictures of the radiant royal parents with their precious new baby, showing him off to the world's press, as she listens to Rita on skype.

"You know we have." Rita replied. "Remember, last summer we went on a trip to Hampton Court. That was built by Wolsey, even though the king got to enjoy it after his death."

"Oh yes," Priya recalled the red brick walls topped by magnificent chimneys and large halls redolent of the Tudor period, the huge fireplaces and kitchens where vast banquets would have been prepared and the long passages through which servants would have hurried with provisions and cooked dishes. Everything was on a massive scale. Wolsey clearly had a high opinion of himself if he thought he should enjoy that level of luxury, not quite in keeping with the modesty of a clergyman Priya thought. She recalled the building being surprisingly tall and elegant for the period and she remembered they were told the walls were lined with rich tapestries. Wolsey had started the building in 1514 and carried on into the 1520s. It was clearly a pet project of his.

"You've seen pictures of him." Rita reminded her friend. "Striding about the court in his long red robes and Cardinal's hat, chains of office round his neck. He certainly seemed to enjoy the trappings of power. He had a patron in Richard Foxe, the Lord Privy Seal, and seems to have impressed early on with hard work, energy and attention to detail. Once, he was sent abroad on an errand and was back before they realised he had been away! He had a reputation of being able to work for twelve hours a day without a break!" Rita said; the girls paused to think about this.

"He was disparaged after his death as the son of a butcher, but that may not be true since his father could afford to send him to Ipswich School and Magdalen School and College. Some people think his father was a cloth merchant, and that his father died at the battle of Bosworth, but who knows? He certainly rose high. Wolsey was accused after his death of imagining himself the equal of kings. When they were plotting his downfall, the King's advisers put together a 'dodgy dossier' showing his excesses but also of course allowing them to cherry- pick his best assets when he did die."

"What were his dates?" Priya indulged her friend.

"1475 or thereabouts to 1530. So he was 55 when he died." ('About the same age as Brian,' Rita thought as she said this.)

"He was a very clever man and good at his job. He was hard working for the King in the early years and made a good statesman for Henry at home and abroad. Failure to get the annulment brought about his downfall, but he was very ambitious and maybe the king would have had enough of him anyway at some point. He gathered church titles and properties all over the country. He started as royal chaplain, then became Bishop of Lincoln and then Archbishop of York before becoming Lord Chancellor of England and Cardinal, Papal Legate. I guess in some ways at that time, because of the authority of the Pope, that gave him more power than Henry. I expect it all went to his head a bit. You remember they told us you had to go through eight rooms to get to his audience chamber. I think he lost touch with reality somewhere along the line!"

"Is that why you are so obsessed with him?" Priya asked.

"It's a classic case of rise and fall, isn't it? And the fact that he died in Leicester." Rita explained.

"Like Richard III!" exclaimed Priya. "Maybe they will try to find Wolsey's body next!"

"Well, they might." said Rita seriously, "I must mention it in my personal statement. They know he was buried in the Lady Chapel, so there's probably a fair chance of locating him. Maybe his bones could reveal whether he was poisoned. He asked the King for 'grace, mercy, remission and pardon' but I think he knew the game was up when the King sent someone from the Tower of London to escort him back south; he could have poisoned himself." she added.

"Have they decided where to bury Richard yet?" Priya asked, getting to the pages in her magazine on Katie Price's latest pregnancy; she had written to Peter Andre's girlfriend, apparently, sending 'genuine congratulations' on the fact that she was pregnant too; Priya wondered why that phrase immediately made her sound not genuine.

"No, I think there might be a court case. Some people want to argue for him to be buried in York." Rita said.

"History is not just about the past, it goes on affecting us today." said Priya.

"Good phrase!" said Rita, noting it down.

* * *

"Could you give the 'hell hole' a clear out please? It hasn't been done for ages." Athena calls from the kitchen.

The girls raise their eyebrows to each other and shrug. It's not a job they enjoy. The hell hole smells of muddy boots and dust. "Ice cream treat later?" Rita suggests to her friend as an incentive "Deal!" says Priya. As they start to lay out the contents of the cupboard in order to clean it, Rita recalls her conversation with Edward, Athena's husband, earlier that day.

* * *

She and Priya had found him standing by the sitting room window, looking out over the front of the house, where the sundial stands, when they entered the room. He was wearing old clothes and shoes and was holding his gardening gloves in one hand and a mug of steaming liquid in the other.

"Hello girls." he had greeted them, "I'm just taking a break." He had raised his mug as evidence. He was balding, with a tonsure of grey hair. Edward was overweight (too

83

many client lunches he explains to Athena when she draws his attention to this) and the overall effect when he sat down was of an ebullient humpty dumpty with spectacles.

"Back for long?" Priya asked as they emptied the waste paper basket and plumped the LIVE, LAUGH, LOVE, PEACE cushions.

"A couple of weeks, hopefully." Edward replied. "It gets very hot out there. You just want to get back and breathe normal air again. Over there it's too hot outside and too cold. With the air conditioning, inside."

"What have you been doing with your clients?" Rita ventured.

"Basically licensing agreements." Edward scratched his head as he explained. "My clients are authorising various companies to market their products. It's high-end beauty treatments – Botox, facial serums, that sort of thing."

"Is there much demand?" Priya wanted to know.

"You'd probably be surprised." Edward said, "Behind those veils the women are very beauty conscious. They want to look their best. And they can afford it."

"You heard what's happened here?" Rita asked, "About Brian Jackson." she amplified.

"Oh yeah. Terrible business." Edward settled back on the leather sofa. The girls tried not to notice the marks on the carpet from his shoes. They would have to clean those up when he went.

"I wanted to ask you a couple of things actually." Rita went on. Priya rolled her eyes to the ceiling and carried on dusting the window seats. ('This may take some time.' she was thinking).

"If someone makes a will and then they get divorced, does the will still count?"

Edward pulled his head back a little, surprised at the question and searching his memory for the law of probate.

"Well yes," he replied slowly. "A divorce won't upset a will.

If you get divorced you need to make sure you make a new will. So your wishes are clear." After a pause he added, "Why? You're not even married are you?" he laughed a little.

"Oh no," Rita clarified, "I was thinking about Brian Jackson. His affairs. What the position might be."

"Oh" said Edward, interested now, and the attractions of lawn-edging temporarily receding "Tell me more."

"OK, Brian inherited some money from his uncle recently." Rita's hands wove around each other like two birds as she spoke.

"And you know this how?" Edward interrupted Rita quickly and suspiciously.

Priya piped up in mitigation on her friend's behalf, "We saw some letters when we were clearing his room. We didn't mean to pry or anything."

"Oh, ok" said Edward, "Do go on."

"Well then there was a letter about the divorce - Brian's second marriage, to Jan. Something called a decree N-I-S-I had come through."

"Not a decree absolute?" Edward clarified. "Nisi means 'unless'; it's an interim step on the road to a full divorce. It allows time for issues like finance to be sorted out."

"Mmm." Rita nodded to indicate this seemed to be the case with Brian, "And the letters also said they were drawing up a new will. But it doesn't look like there was time for that to happen."

"Let me get this straight." Edward had put down his mug and was rubbing his hand over his bald patch; he spread out his fingers as if pointing to an imaginary map.

"Brian inherits. Brian gets a decree nisi. Brian is changing his will but had not done it when he died?" he leant back against the sofa.

"I think so." said Rita, adding, "Who would benefit in those circumstances?"

Priya was standing still by the window, listening for

Edward's answer. 'Was Rita on to something?' she was thinking.

"It's a bit of a pickle, then." was Edward's considered opinion after a short silence. "I'm not an expert and it's a long time since I did this. But suppose, suppose." He started to count off points with his fingers, "Suppose he had a will which left everything to his second wife, the one he was married to most recently. If there was no decree absolute, and no will change, then she inherits; but suppose he had revoked his will and not made a new one, then she inherits if he dies before the decree absolute, if he dies after, then his other relatives – his sons I guess – would inherit. Of course, we don't know if there was an existing will or what the will said. He might have left it to the local church or the cats home for all we know."

"So we need to know whether there was a will and what it says?" Rita clarified. (Priya was thinking, 'Who is 'we' here?') "And you're not properly divorced until the decree absolute?" Rita added.

"Mmmn" Edward confirmed, "A lot of people don't realise that." He added before picking up his mug, draining the rest of his coffee into his throat and placing the mug back on the table, leaving a wet ring for Rita and Priya to clear up. ('I can see who Morwenna takes after.' thinks Rita.)

"Back to pruning and edging for me," and he made his muddy trail back across the room, pausing to add as he turned, smiling, towards the door, "Oh, and of course, if a relative did it then they can't inherit. You can't benefit from your crime." he had added before he disappeared, leaving the impression of his grin behind him, like the Cheshire cat, and leaving Rita and Priya to clear up in his wake.

* * *

"Take Henry" Rita pushes the hoover out of the 'hell hole'

towards her friend. Rita is now like Aladdin, inside the cave, with Priya as Jafar on the outside. She dives into the cupboard for the next objects, which is the croquet mallets and hoops, followed by the footballs and croquet balls. A few assorted sun hats, wellingtons and gardening gloves later, plus tennis rackets and balls, a couple of rugs and a sun shade, and the cupboard is empty.

The girls use Henry to clean the cupboard floor and spray polish on the door. This improves the odour considerably.

"Strange." says Priya as they start to re-fill the space.

"Mmmn?" Rita is distracted, thinking about Edward's information.

"There's usually a wheelchair in here isn't there? Has someone borrowed it?"

When Rita and Priya have finished their task they go to find Athena to see if there are any more jobs before they leave. They are planning a trip into the town centre and are looking forward to the ice cream they have promised themselves. They find Athena in the dining room and the three settle to talk for a few minutes, savouring the peace of the place.

Rita tells Athena about her visit to the Temple on her day off yesterday. She had been with Mohal to take some flowers and think about Brian. "You aren't supposed to ask the gods for things" she explains to Athena, "But you can't help asking. I did express the hope that Brian is at peace and happy".

They talk a little about life as a continuous journey or circle and Priya asks Athena what she thinks about when she meditates. "I have various sayings that I like to repeat, she explains, one of my favourites is –

'May everyone be happy,
May everyone be free from misery,
May no one ever be separated from their happiness,
May everyone have equanimity,
Free from hatred and attachment.'".

Just as she finishes, her mobile ring tone intrudes into

their quiet time. Athena pulls an apologetic face when she sees the caller, as if to say "I can't ignore it." The girls go into the kitchen, wipe down the surfaces and clean away the crumbs from breakfast while they wait. They listen attentively to see if they can make out who Athena is talking to but she has moved to the sitting room now and no sounds carry through the door, which she has closed. They have just cleaned everything they can think of when Athena finally gets off the phone and comes in.

"Sorry, sorry." she apologises and sinks onto one of the dining chairs, breathing out deeply like someone who's just finished a difficult task. Priya puts the kettle on.

"Problem?" Rita encourages from the kitchen.

"Not for me." says Athena brightly "For poor Cynthia."

Priya looks at Rita, puzzled, Rita mouths silently "Brian's first wife." Priya nods her understanding.

"She rang about the Memorial - we're arranging it in the Park to commemorate Brian."

"What about it?" Priya places Earl Grey tea before their boss and goes back to make mint tea for herself and Rita, who is also now sitting at the table; ice cream, Priya realises, will have to wait.

"Cynthia's had a call from the solicitor. The one dealing with Brian's affairs. Or she rang him. I can't remember now." Athena takes a sip of her tea. "Anyway, the point is she's very upset. Brian said he would give her money to help with the cost of Simon's education. You know she wants to send him to a specialist College, preferably for him to board, so he'll be like other lads of his age?"

"Well?" Rita is leaning forward over the mug Priya has placed before her before on the table.

"He hasn't. That's the problem. He didn't give her any money before he died and his will leaves everything to Jan, his second wife. Cynthia doesn't know what to do. She's in a terrible state. She doesn't know what provision to make for

Simon now. And he should be starting in September. The college and the education authority have agreed he can have a place but social services don't have anything in their budget to pay for his accommodation. It's the cutbacks because of the recession I suppose."

"Oh dear." Rita says sympathetically. "Was Brian going to make a payment then?"

"She says he was, she says he was committed to helping Simon if he could. It's all come at just the wrong time. It's awful for her. Poor woman!"

"Bad luck." says Priya. "Will they be at the Memorial?"

"I hope so." Athena says. "Most of the family should be there, and the actors. You are coming aren't you?" she asks the girls and they nod their confirmation. The Memorial will take place in Abbey Park in a few days' time, all being well, followed by refreshments at Sundial.

Chapter

10

"No warmth, no breath shall testify thou livest; the roses in thy lips and cheek shall fade to wanny ashes, thy eyes' windows fall. Like death when he shuts up the day of life."

Friar Laurence in
Romeo and Juliet
by Shakespeare.

Wednesday August 7th 2013

"What a mean thing to do!"

Priya has called Rita on her i-phone. It is late in the evening and Rita is in her bedroom, lying on the pink duvet cover, looking out of her window to the street and dark sky beyond. The night is clear and warm and she has her window partially open to allow air to circulate. She has been looking again at her personal statement. It seems to Rita that the more she tries to improve it, the worse it gets. Why are you applying to university? (duh!) Why have you chosen that subject? (Where to start?). Then there's the tricky bit about relating your extra-curricular activities to your proposed course. How to make cleaning a bed and breakfast sound like it's related to history? And everything has to be fitted into to 47 lines or less. She was polishing a sentence that began "History is one of the most important things in my life. I have read widely and am interested in the lives of ordinary people from the past and the impact of their lives on current events and situations."

Rita saves this and puts her friend on loudspeaker so they can talk while she opens her iPad.

"I know, it's terrible what people post on twitter. That woman just wanted Jane Austen on the bank notes. She doesn't deserve those threats." (The girls are discussing the freelance journalist from Rutland who led the on-line campaign and has been in the local press and on television about the threats she has received.)

"History affecting life again!" says Priya, then "Oh, have you heard from Athena?"

Rita is more alert now. She senses from her friend's tone that there is news about Brian Jackson's death.

"Athena phoned me. She wants our help over the weekend. Some of Brian's family are coming to stay on Sunday night ready for the Memorial. She says she's finding it hard to keep it all together." Priya adds.

Rita thinks quickly. "Yes, the weekend should be ok." She wants to go to Sundial as their help has not been needed for the past few days and she wonders if there have been developments. This week she has been busy at home, having been deputed by her parents to keep an eye on her brother Nayan. Today was easy as they were doing a Creepy House theme at St Barnabas library as part of the summer reading challenge. If you visited the library 6 times to borrow and read books you got stickers and a glow in the dark wrist band. Nayan had managed this easily and was especially pleased with the creepy face paints which had been applied to his features and which had scared Rita when he leered round the corner at her. It was a pity that Leicestershire were not playing cricket at home that week, Rita had thought, as this would have kept Nayan safely occupied. He is excited that the Leicestershire captain Matthew Hoggard, is due to appear on Celebrity Masterchef soon ("I hope he doesn't drop anything." Nayan says).

"What's the trouble?" Rita is intrigued.

"The Inspector has been back. He checked through Sundial and Athena's flat. She wasn't happy. Apparently they are looking for morphine."

"Morphine?" Rita's voice rises, she is nonplussed "Why?" she writes the new information into her notes straight away.

"More toxicology results apparently. Brian had morphine in his system."

"So he was drugged?" Rita checks.

"Looks like it?" Priya replies questioningly.

"Well, how was it administered? Was that injected too?"

"It seems it was in his stomach, Athena said. Probably mixed with the wine he drank."

Both girls go silent, recalling the glasses and the wine bottle they cleared from Brian's room.

"Did we mention the wine and the bottle to Inspector Bridge?" Rita asks her friend at last.

"I don't remember. We should make sure he knows." Priya replies.

"So someone must have planned this. Must have arranged to drug Brian and then inject him? Who would hate him that much?" Rita was still thinking about this as she got ready for bed later.

* * *

"Was Brian in touch with friends from the old days?" she had asked Cynthia in the dining room when Inspector Bridge had finished talking to her and Brian's mother, explaining that "He told me what it was like to go down the mine."

"Oh aye," Cynthia had said "Not that most of the men were friends if you get my meaning. The strike caused a lot of bad feeling. First there were the ones that wanted to go back, some even travelled to collieries in Nottingham and joined them. That included Brian's brother, Ian." She paused for a moment, as if digging deep into memories she had tried to bury. "I suppose he was desperate." Another pause. "He worked at Thorseby, as far as I know. I kept in touch with his wife for a while, but secretly, so Brian wouldn't know; he was very bitter. Scabs were hated for strike-breaking and the feeling was mutual. They resented the ones who stuck it out. Felt they were keeping food from other families' mouths. Especially as there was never a national ballot. Then, after the strike, when the Grimethorpe colliery was being run down, that caused bad feeling. Some got jobs elsewhere, some didn't, Some of the men resented Brian his chance at modelling and then acting. His mother had comments daubed on the house at one point. I used to worry they'd actually attack him – you know-spoil his looks for the sake of it. All that community spirit gone!" she had lamented.

"But Brian said he could handle himself." she went on "So yes, he knew blokes in Grimethorpe, but there weren't many happy reunions. He didn't set foot in the miners' social club once he started on the modelling lark. So why did he stay in Grimethorpe? It were Margaret."

Cynthia had glanced in the direction of the sitting room where her ex mother in law was sitting. Rita thought she had better not mention Brian's brother to Margaret. That was clearly a closed subject as far as she was concerned.

"Margaret is Grimethorpe born and bred. Her father went down the pit and his before that. She wouldn't move and Brian wouldn't leave without her, not while he and I were married any road." Cynthia had added, "We'd been childhood sweethearts, married at 19, and we lived a couple of doors down from his mother." she paused.

"After we broke up, and he took up with Jan, he lived in Nottingham," she made it sound as exotic as New York or New Orleans, "When that marriage broke down, after the TV work dried up, I s'pose it made sense for him to go back to be with Margaret again, when he wasn't working." she finished.

Rita falls asleep recalling something else Athena said when they were talking together last week. That the truth would be known. She used one of her Buddhist sayings "Three things cannot be hidden; the sun, the moon and the truth."

* * *

Thursday August 8th 2013

"Pass the biscuits." Priya, Rita and Nayan are in a café near Leicester market the next day. Nayan has been with the girls to Sundial ('I'd be fine on my own!' he protested) where they quickly dusted and cleaned to remove signs of the police search the day before. The café is his reward. Nayan is playing premier league on his Nintendo and tucking into the wafer biscuits. He and his friends are texting about the new football season which is about to start; Nigel Pearson, the Leicester manager has said he has all the players he wants for the season. Nayan particularly likes the Leicester goal keeper, Kasper Schmeichel. 'Maybe this is the year that City will get promotion to the Premier League!' he thinks (Nayan was four years old when Leicester were last in the top league, so he has no memory of this).

The girls have their lap tops open and are supposed to be polishing their draft personal statements; they will be able to finalise them when they have their AS results and the applications will refer to predictions for their A levels next year. Priya, having spotted the news that the Richard III Visitor Centre has been given the go-ahead ("Well, we'll see" is Rita's comment back) is on Facebook checking out the status of various school friends. Rita is on line gathering what information she can on Marina and Ash. The new information about the morphine makes Brian's death all the more suspicious; 'can they really have had nothing to do with it?' she thinks.

"Why are you interested in them?" Priya had made the mistake of asking. As her friend begins to run through her

94

theories, Priya reaches for her comb to run through her hair.

"What if Ash didn't just close Brian's door. What it he went in, drugged and killed him? It would explain why Ash didn't want Marina to tell the police he was there."

"But why would be he do that?" Nayan looks up. "You need Motive as well as Opportunity." He adds, recalling dialogue from an episode of Law and Order he saw recently.

"I don't know. An argument they had. Or jealousy. Maybe Brian made a pass at Marina."

"Unlikely?" Priya is sceptical.

"Ok then." Rita acknowledges, "Well, what if they were both in on it?"

"How?" Priya queries.

"What if they asked Brian to join them in a bottle of wine, got him drunk and killed him."

"Again," Priya sighs, leaning on her elbows, "Why?"

"Same motive. Or something else we don't know about."

"Could they have done it, assuming they had a motive?" Nayan raises his head to speak again, his mouth full of wafer biscuit, remembering that 'Means' is the third aspect that needs to be established according to the crime programmes he watches.

"Ash shares a room with Jacob who is diabetic; so Ash would have access to insulin, assuming that's what Jacob takes." Rita makes a note to find this out. "And Marina has worked in a beauty clinic – I bet she knows how to inject Botox – what's the difference?"

"It all sounds very premeditated." Priya objects, "And if it was them, why suddenly tell the truth? No one would have known Ash was at Sundial if Marina hadn't said."

"Good point," Rita concedes, "Maybe they thought they were seen? Or might be found out? So it was better to come clean?"

"My head hurts," says Priya, sipping the raspberry tea in front of her.

"Can we think about alibis? Who definitely couldn't have done it?" she suggests.

"Hardly anyone has an alibi if you think about it." her friend rejoins, "Of course it depends on when you think it happened. The police seem pretty vague about that. Brian seems to have died sometime between twelve midnight and six in the morning."

"Mmmn." Priya stares at her screen.

"Athena was alone in her flat-" Rita begins.

"You're not thinking it might be her?" Priya is startled.

"Got to rule everyone in or out. You and me included." Rita says.

Priya is outraged "I was home with my parents!"

"Me too. OK that was easy." Rita pretends to tick their names off an imaginary list.

"Then there's where…" Rita presses on. "Let's look at my time line." She refers to her notes. Nayan leaves the table to get himself another drink. As he gets up Rita thinks, "Has he grown again? He looks taller than yesterday!"

"He had changed his clothes, so he came back to Sundial after the play - Athena saw him come back. Aaran said he was going to meet someone after the play. Who was that? Caroline? A new girlfriend? Maybe even his brother, if they were in touch? Was he injected at Sundial or at the Park?"

Rita is making notes as she speaks, her personal statement forgotten.

"Ash and Marina alibi each other up to six o'clock on Tuesday morning and have lied or been 'economical with the truth' already. Jacob, Ash's roommate had no alibi for the relevant time if Ash was with Marina." She summarises.

"Caroline is staying in the same house as Ash and Jacob. The female actors are together in another bed and breakfast. Surely the police will have questioned their whereabouts?" Rita thinks aloud.

"What about the family? Brian's mother is also diabetic

but presumably can be ruled out as being (a) too old and (b) too far away. She doesn't seem to have any transport unless someone brings her. Cynthia seems to have her hands full with Simon, although she looks pretty strong. Jan lives and works in Nottingham as does Brian's brother, Ian." Rita continues.

"If Brian was drunk or drugged, how did he get to the Park?" Nayan asks. Priya looks at him with respect; he is paying attention to his sister's musings! she thinks.

"Yes. Who would have done that and how? That's the question to ask." Rita agrees.

"Marina has a car, as does Athena, Cynthia, Caroline and Jan. But Brian's own car was at the Park so presumably he drove himself? Or was driven in it? Or he did not come back to Sundial in it and someone else moved it? But then how did they get his keys?" Rita wracks her brains for what Athena said she remembered of the Monday evening.

"A car, about 11pm. Two people on the steps, a man and a woman, she in a long skirt, he in jeans and desert boots, the same desert boots that Brian wore."

But Marina said she came back at 11pm. Since Marina was entertaining Ash, Rita wonders if the people that Athena saw could have been Marina and Ash? Ash wears desert boots just like Brian's. Would Athena have failed to hear Marina's car arriving, with its distinctive engine? Athena did say she had been meditating, so maybe she was not alert to the car engine? In that case, when did Brian get back and was it with a woman or someone else? Rita starts to think as she doodles circles on a napkin. What did Marina and Ash hear? She strains to recall. Someone saying "Goodnight Brian" (so he did have a visitor; but Marina had not said whether it was the voice of a man or a woman?) and Ash had heard a mechanical noise. Rita's doodled circles are overlapping and forming new shapes. What did it all mean?

Chapter

11

"Peace, ho, for shame! confusion's cure lives not In these confusions."

Friar Laurence in
Romeo and Juliet
by Shakespeare.

Friday August 9th 2013 (morning)

Sitting, after her breakfast of cornflakes and orange juice, at the table in her mother's kitchen – designer white cupboards and granite work tops- Rita is comparing street maps of Leicester, York and Oxford. Mr Thatcher had told them you can find out a lot about an area's story by the names given to the roads. She knew, of course, that The Shambles in York had been home to butchers' shops and houses and derived from the Flemish 'shamel' meaning booth or bench, or 'flesshammel', a butcher's bench. Tanner Row in York was a give-away as were Horsefair Street in Leicester and Beef Lane and Brewer Street in Oxford.

In York, she had learned, the ending 'gate' such as Coppergate and Deangate meant 'street' from the Viking 'gatta', while the gateways through the walls were called 'bars' (Bootham Bar, Monk Bar, Walmgate Bar and Micklegate Bar). Leicester, too, had 'gates' meaning streets, such as Churchgate and Gallowtree Gate, which spoke of a gruesome past. There were quirky names on the maps like Turn Again Lane in Oxford and Whipmawhopmagate in York. Other road names showed the previous presence of closed monasteries and convents, such as Greyfriars in Leicester, Nunnery Lane in York and Old Greyfriars Street in Oxford.

Rita calls Priya on skype to tell her that she had bumped into Judith the day before in the town centre, and to see if her friend can come round later.

"Can you see the sniper?" Nayan's voice from the sitting room can be heard by Priya as the girls try to have a conversation.

"What's Nayan saying?" Priya asks.

"He's gaming and stuff." says Rita "Online, with his friend."

"Nayan has a friend?" Priya says, incredulous.

"Yeah, they're going to see the Lone Ranger film with Johnny Depp at the weekend. I thought you might come round later and watch a DVD or something on Netflix? Nayan will be at football".

"I'll see if I can get a lift… What are you doing?" Priya asks her friend who has moved to the kitchen drawers.

"Looking for a long spoon. I want to make hot chocolate with that set I got for my birthday."

"Mmmn" says Priya appreciatively. "Marshmallows?"

"Natch!" Rita replies, then "Ah!" as she finds the spoon she is looking for.

"Decided on your Uni choices yet?" Priya asks

"Nope. The parents are pushing Leicester – it has one of the largest History Departments in the country…"

"And it would be cheaper!" Priya interrupts.

"Mmmn. At York you can study in small groups, though, and maybe study abroad for a year."

"Would you like to do that?" Priya is unsure about this.

"I might. Warwick offers that too, especially American history; I'm enjoying that aspect and might want to do more. Have you come to any conclusions yet?"

"I think Birmingham or Leicester, unless I get an offer from Oxford." Priya says. "I don't think I would like to live in London, it's too big."

"Well, I'll visit you wherever you are." says Rita.

"So, come on, spill." Priya changes the subject. "What did

Judith tell you?"

"Well," says Rita, "It was quite interesting actually."

Rita had met Judith by chance the previous day in Marks and Spencer's food department in the town centre. Judith, it turned out, was one of those people who does not let a chance to gossip go by, even if it means standing between the fish and dessert sections of the food shop and causing an obstruction with her large presence.

"Hello Rita." Judith had made the first move. Rita had not recognised the actor that day as she was out of context and wrapped in large black and white stripes which met in an alarming way round Judith's ample middle. The effect was that of a zebra crossing that had melted, or been twisted out of shape in an earthquake. ('Why do they design such things for larger women?' Rita thought. 'It just draws attention to their size.')

"Hi Judith." Rita had replied, "I'm here with my brother. He's just gone to get biscuits." she explained, adding "How are things?"

Judith had taken this as a cue to describe in some detail the emotional temperature of the Company in general and each actor in particular, who was bearing up and who was depressed. It helped, apparently, that Romeo and Juliet had ended its run, since memories of Brian's performance in it could be dispelled. But a new play had brought new challenges and everyone was aware that memories of Brian would haunt them, at least until they moved on from Leicester.

Of the men in the Dragon Company, Jacob and Ash seemed the most shaken, Judith told Rita, ignoring the pleading features of a woman with a full basket and a toddler at her side who was trying to squeeze by. Jacob kept saying he could not believe it and that he expected Brian to walk on stage any moment. "Good job we're not doing Macbeth or Hamlet where there are ghosts in the play." Judith had said. Ash was upset he had not been able to do more when he found Brian. He'd never seen a dead body before so he found the experience very disturbing. Ash had missed a couple of lighting cues the previous night, apparently, so there was an extra technical rehearsal taking place as they spoke, hence Judith had time to gossip in Marks and Spencer.

Rita had looked round for Nayan and spotted him out of the corner of her eye. It looked like he had paid for the biscuits and was keeping out of Rita's way until the coast was clear.

"Caroline is very cut up, of course." Judith was saying, "Not only has this made extra work for her – changing the programmes, that sort of thing - but also, of course, she and Brian were an item earlier this year."

"An item?" Priya is intrigued. "She said that?"

"Apparently." Rita replies. "I don't know how he had the time for it in between rehearsals. And after breaking up with his wife."

"Mmmn, especially tricky being with someone in the Company." Priya contributes.

"Exactly." Rita agrees, "Who would Brian complain to if he wasn't happy about the management of the tour for example?"

"When was his break-up?" Priya wants to know.

"I asked Judith that. She thought they separated last summer - 2012." Rita answers.

"And he started seeing Caroline when?" Priya is formulating an idea.

"It was on and off for about 6 months according to Judith. It started around last autumn and finished in the spring."

"Do you think Caroline caused the break-up? Brian didn't waste much time!" Priya observes. She is in her bedroom at her home, trying not to disturb her mother who is downstairs on the computer arranging deliveries to customers for her on-line clothes business. If Priya lets her get on with it she may drive her daughter to Rita's house later, she thinks.

"I don't suppose Caroline is Jan's favourite person." says Rita, recalling the look on Jan's face as she watched the croquet game in May.

"Did you kill him?" Nayan's excited voice from the sitting room interrupts the girls' conversation again (he is using the wide-screen wall-mounted television to give himself the best view of the snipers he wants to shoot).

"Yes!" a triumphant tone this time. "That will get us to the next level!" Rita's brother exclaims.

"Did they give any reason when they split up?" Priya asks when Nayan's noise subsides.

"Judith didn't seem to think so. She just thought they drifted apart."

"And what about the fight Judith saw, in Doncaster, did she tell you any more about that?" asks Priya, guessing that her friend would have tried to use the conversation to get more information.

"Oh yes, I asked her about the miners' strike, actually, in case she had any memories but she said she was abroad at the time. But she did think the fight was connected with it. She had the impression that Brian and his opponent knew each other from his mining days. And she remembered something else, that the other bloke had large tattoos on his arms and neck." Rita tells her.

"Well that may not narrow it down much." Priya observes unhelpfully. "Unless we know what the tattoos looked like. Everyone has them these days. I blame David Beckham."

"Mmmn. You're so right." says Rita, then "I'm thinking of going to see someone who remembers the miners' strike, if Mohal will take me; I'll ask if he will pick you up as well."

"Oh, OK." says Priya, trying to sound casual, then "When are you starting driving lessons?" she asks Rita, changing the subject.

"Maybe at half term?" Rita replies, "If my parents think I'm doing OK at school."

"Oh, there's Mohal now," she adds, hearing the front door being opened. "I'll see if he'll give me a lift and fetch you over. Laters!"

"Laters!" the girls sign off.

* * *

Friday 9th August 2013 (afternoon)

Rita finds Richard Gregson in the lounge of the nursing home in Thurmaston where Mohal has dropped her off before going to Loughborough to fetch Priya ("Am I your personal chauffeur or what?" he said, but Rita had pointed out that Nayan needed taking to football and Priya's house was not too far out of Mohal's way).

Mr Gregson used to own the house next door to Rita's, before he and his wife moved away from the area. He was once a City councillor and Rita had met him when she was doing a project on the arrival in Leicester of Asians from Uganda in the 1970s. Rita thinks he may have memories of the miners' strike, which Brian had mentioned, and, anyway, she had enjoyed their previous chat. Richard Gregson may not have a good short term memory any more, but his recall of the past was still very sharp Rita recalled.

Mr Gregson is seated on an upright chair and his moustachioed face broadens into a smile when he sees Rita.

"Hello!" he warmly greets her. "How's Elm Drive today?"

"Oh it's fine." says Rita, "Mr and Mrs Sharma are in your house now. They're very nice. You would like them." Rita says about their newest neighbours. Like Mr Gregson and his wife, the Sharmas have no children. Rita realises this means that, since Mr Gregson's wife has died, he has few visitors. No wonder he is pleased to see her.

A health care worker called Moira appears, and offers to put Richard Gregson in a wheelchair so Rita can take him into the garden, the weather being sunny and warm. Mr Gregson agrees and she expertly helps him into the chair, using her weight and his to balance themselves, like a complicated ballroom dance. ("We're supposed to have two people to do this," Moira says, "But it takes too long and we're short staffed. The sun would have gone by the time we got organised!" she adds, smiling.)

Safely installed in his wheelchair, Mr Gregson permits Rita to propel him out of the glass doors and on to the terrace. She finds this is surprisingly easy as Richard Gregson did not look a lightweight.

"What do you remember about the miners' strike?" she asks him when they have chosen their spot to sit and admire the gardens which are teeming with bright colour- red, pink and orange fountains among lakes of greenery.

"The 1980s?" Mr Gregson says. "Well I do remember, yes." he goes on "As councillors, we were very concerned. We wanted to support the miners as best we could. They were Labour members too. But it was difficult because there'd been no national ballot. Neil Kinnock, national Labour leader at the time, had to sound sympathetic but couldn't give full official support because of the lack of a ballot. Towards the end, he was making a lot of noises about compromise and going back with dignity. Kinnock was Welsh of course and there were lots of miners in Wales who were suffering because of the strike. I think Mr Kinnock knew the game was up long before Arthur Scargill, the miners' leader, would admit it." he shuffled a bit in his chair.

"The trouble was the strike went on for so long. A whole year. I expect at the beginning the workers thought the Government would cave in, like Mr Heath, the Prime Minister, did in the 1970s. But Mrs Thatcher was made of different metal. People say she planned to bring the miners down. I'm not so sure about that, but she made sure the country was ready for a strike and she was as stubborn and determined as Arthur was. There were horrible battles between the strikers and the police – like at Orgreave when they virtually carried out a cavalry charge and Arthur got hit on the head – that made the TV news headlines. Many on the Tory side wanted Mrs Thatcher to end it but she kept on. Well, they always present it as the Coal Board against the miners but of course everybody knew the Government was pulling the strings. The strike would have had a greater effect, for example, if the police hadn't intervened so much – ensuring that flying pickets couldn't get around the country and that working miners could get into the collieries and so forth. One word from number 10 and Mr MacGregor, the Coal Board Chairman, would have changed his tack I'm sure, for a price no doubt." he pauses to take a drink of water from the glass which Moira has brought over.

"But as it turned out the strike achieved nothing except what the Conservatives probably wanted all along, a weakened miners' union which enabled them to close pits and privatise what was left of the coal industry." he sighs. "We tried as a council to provide what support we could to the Leicestershire mineworkers but we were very constrained. We couldn't use council funds for political purposes. We had to provide money through the Labour party and the unions. The other trade unions offered support at the beginning but that dwindled as the strike wore on. People questioned what the NUM had done with the money it received. They were made bankrupt after a couple of their members won a court case alleging the strike was illegal. NUM funds were seized and some were sent abroad to avoid this, I think. After that, there were a lot of secret deals and meetings in lay-bys, money in brown envelopes if you know what I mean. But a union can't go on like that for too long." He finishes.

"What about after the strike? When the men went back?" Rita asks.

"The local councils sensed there would be job losses and

change in the long run. They tried to get some regeneration money into the areas affected. Some open cast areas made good wetlands for wildlife, while Snibston was used as an industrial museum. It all takes time to change, mind." he adds. "Lots of men never got over it. Stayed on benefits for the rest of their lives."

They talk a little about the gardens around them and Rita tells Mr Gregson about her father's garden, which he says he would like to see some day. Then Rita wheels him back inside in time for his evening meal. What she has learnt about the strike fitted with Brian's description, Rita thinks. Had his past caught up with him, she wonders? Did the answer to his death lie in his past? She is thinking as she waits for Mohal, with Priya in his car, to collect her.

Chapter

12

"The grey eyed morn frowns on the shining night."
Friar Lawrence in
Romeo and Juliet
by Shakespeare

Thursday August 15th 2013

Early in the day, when they went to school to see their friends get their A level results, the sky was streaked with colour and looked as if silver and pink ribbons had been trailed across it. Maybe the good weather is going to break, Rita had thought. But the day has turned out bright and the light sharp. Rita is glad she has remembered her sunglasses. She sits as casually as you can in a boat, on the lake, the lake where Brian Jackson's body was found over 3 weeks ago. Rita is conscious not to shift her weight around too much or Mohal, who is operating the pedalo, will get annoyed. She looks across at Priya, whose stiff body and clenched hands betray her nervousness. Priya is not a good swimmer or confident in water; she has only come along because Mohal is there and she never misses an opportunity to be near him.

Nayan is behind Mohal, at the front of the boat (Rita thinks there is probably a special word for 'front' but does not know what it is). Nayan is waiting impatiently for Mohal to hand over the controls. The sky is a cloudless blue; you could make a sari from it, as Padma would say. It is just after lunchtime, so the sun is high and to the south. Shadows are short.

At school that morning they witnessed an emotional atmosphere which was like a combination of a party and a wake as their friends in the year above them collected their A level results and rejoiced expansively in the middle of the room and outside the building, or commiserated quietly in corners, with staff on hand to help the most crestfallen. Reporters from the Leicester Mercury, the local paper, had been there, so it was likely that pictures of their friends would appear in the press that evening. Rita and Priya had looked with a mixture of envy and anticipation at the A level students in their last incarnation as school pupils and thought "that will be us next year!" with excitement and awe.

"Next year we'll be having our prom." Rita says, voicing the thoughts the girls had earlier about what it will be like to be in their final year. "It's not all it's cracked up to be." Mohal puts in with the voice of experience. "Lots of fuss over nothing if you ask me." Rita and Priya exchange a despairing look.

Office workers are gathered on the banks watching with envy those with time to go out on the lake. They munch sandwiches or salads, mostly purchased from the café or a nearby shop, and twist open plastic drink bottles or snap off ring pulls on cans. They look hot in their office wear - jackets, heeled shoes. The women stretch out their legs, some aiming to improve their tan, others glad of the chance to stretch their limbs after hours in front of computer screens or talking on the phone. Some of the men also stretch out, lying flat on the ground, while others sit with their knees up, backs slightly hunched, eyes screwed up to view the lake and the horizon.

Other boats convey young people – school kids, college and university students – and some older people. The older couples negotiate their way carefully around the lake, skippered by husbands (Rita presumes) experienced at manoeuvring around the more erratic, exuberant and unpredictable crews of young people. Every now and again the tranquil air is pierced with shouts or screams as some calamity occurs or is narrowly averted in a boat of students.

Nayan is trailing a hand in the water. "Imagine what that man found!" he says enthusiastically.

"What man?" Priya chooses to indulge him, as his siblings are bored with his tall tales.

"It said on the news. A man was dredging a pond and got the shock of his life when he found a grenade."

"A grenade?!" Priya is alarmed.

"He'd already found loads of ammunition." Nayan says casually.

"Where was it from?" Priya wants to know.

"This pond was in Lutterworth. The ammunition was very old. Some of it dating back to the First World War. It must have been dumped there I suppose." Nayan explains.

Priya looks around her, even more anxious now. Could there be ammunition in the lake?

"Do they do rowing at your University?" Priya asks Mohal to change the subject, she recalls the hive of activity on the Isis the day she and Rita visited Oxford. From Folly Bridge they watched what seemed like dozens of college boats turning and returning to go past the boat houses towards Iffley lock. The boat houses were identifiable with the colleges by their coats of arms and symbols, just like the Montagu and Capulet families would have been identified by their coats of arms, Priya thinks, recalling the play they had been to see.

"They have a team, but they are not very good." Mohal says in answer to her question. "It's not easy to get to practice."

"I prefer the rowing machine in the gym." says Nayan keenly "You can go as fast as you like."

"And no risk of getting wet!" adds Rita as Nayan and Mohal start to swap places and the boat wobbles precariously on the water's surface.

At that moment, Morwenna floats by, Ophelia-like, her fingers trailing in the cool water while a good looking young man glides their boat onwards. Morwenna affects not to notice Rita and Priya, who reciprocate the gesture.

"Looking forward to the Mela?" Priya asks Rita, anxious to have something to think about apart from the boat sinking. "Yeah." replies her friend, "Mum says we can all four go together." This is good news for Priya as it means she can spend more time in Mohal's company. Thousands are expected for the bank holiday weekend finale of the City festival when there would be crowds and music and food stretching across the town centre from Humberstone Gate to the Market Place. It would be great fun if last year was anything to go by, Rita thinks.

"Preeya Kalidas is supposed to be coming." Mohal says jerkily, alarmed at the way Nayan is standing up in the boat. "Who's she?" Nayan asks to a chorus of "Oh Nayan!" from the girls. Rita explains, "You know, she played Amira Massood in Eastenders. She's a singer."

"And really pretty." Priya adds.

"Do you remember, the Mela used to be in this park." says Mohal. "About 6 or 7 years ago. So you would have been very young." he tells them, reminding the boat members that he is the oldest. "The celebrations got too big, so they moved it to the City centre." he adds.

"No mucking about." the older brother admonishes the younger as he takes over piloting the pedalo. Nayan takes a few attempts to get into a rhythm, anxious to show he can go faster than his brother. When he settles to a steadier movement, Rita relaxes again and stares back at the bank. All evidence of the police activity is gone and they have not heard from Inspector Bridge for several days, not since he searched Athena's flat and Sundial, having revealed that Brian was drugged with morphine, as well as killed with insulin.

'Who would have been able to do that,' Rita is thinking. 'A pharmacist with a grudge would fit the bill, how else to get hold of morphine?' she and Priya had discussed this the day before.

* * *

"Morphine," Priya said. "Well that's a problem to get. It's a controlled drug. Doctors don't prescribe it except to very ill patients and if you collect it you have to sign a special form."

"What does it look like?" Rita wanted to know.

"Well I think you can get it in any form." Priya was interested now. "You can have a liquid – oramorph it's called- or tablets –morphine sulphate is common- or a powder."

"And does it dissolve easily?" Rita had asked.

"I believe so. For patients who can't swallow easily they use a liquid infusion in a drip. Sometimes patients can adjust their dose themselves, within limits obviously. That's what would happen to someone who was very ill." Priya added.

"Would you need much to knock you out?" Rita wanted to know next.

"Probably not a huge amount," Priya thought. "Especially if you weren't already taking morphine. So you weren't used to its effects."

"Brian wasn't ill so he wouldn't be taking morphine," Rita said

"And there was none in his room when we cleared it – no medication apart from a throat spray" Priya confirmed.

"So someone gave it to him. Why? So they could inject him?" Rita thought out loud.

* * *

In the boat Rita, as she recalls their conversation, is thinking, 'it seems like someone must have gone to a lot of trouble and planned Brian's murder in advance.' As she muses on who this might be, Rita realises that a figure walking on the edge of the lake reminds her of someone. It is a tall man with cropped grey hair wearing a vest top, but the distinctive thing about him is the tattoo which can been seen spreading over his neck and chest. Rita has seen photos of those tattoos in the newspaper cuttings at the library. It is Brian's brother, Ian, she is sure of it. What is he doing in Leicester? Ian seems to be strolling alone, looking out at the lake from time to time. Has he just come to see where his brother died? Or is there a more sinister reason?

"Look out for the island," Mohal advises his brother as they come close to a patch of ground which the recent dry weather has exposed in the middle of the lake, and around which moorhens are starting to settle, seeing this as a desirable summer residence.

Everything happens quickly. Mohal is gesticulating at the bank they are approaching, as if by waving his hands it will move away; Nayan tries to turn the boat, but acts too quickly and the boat rocks to one side, almost tipping Nayan out with it, while the girls, alerted by Mohal's shout, hang on to the sides and hope to stay safe.

"Oh Nayan!" Priya suddenly shouts excitedly – he has splashed her accidentally as his hand caught on something in the water. Priya is more surprised than soaked.

"Sorry." Nayan apologises as he straightens himself, struggling to haul up with him whatever it is he has touched in the water. Rita expects to see weeds entangled round her brother's arm, but instead it is a plastic carrier bag. Nayan is about to throw it back in when Rita says, "No." and "Let's have a look." Priya rolls her eyes. What now?

"Oh Rita," Priya says, not liking the idea of a wet slippery bag sharing the cramped space in the boat. She glimpses with her friend into the bag and gasps to see a shirt wrapped round an object that may be (maybe?) a syringe.

"Take us back to the shore," Rita says excitedly to her brother. "Inspector Bridge will want to see this."

* * *

112

"What was in the bag?" a tired Athena wants to know when they call in at Sundial later that afternoon.

"The police took out a shirt – I'm sure it was Brian's - and a syringe, they put everything in an evidence bag. They weren't very happy with how wet it was. It was dripping all over their desk!" Rita tells her.

"I wonder how they missed it when they searched." Athena says, offering them all glasses of lemonade and home-made cookies. Nayan helps himself eagerly. ('He needs food with all that growing', thinks Rita.)

"Strange what they find and what they don't." says Athena. "They've taken away all my baking ingredients and make up! As if I could hide anything like morphine there!"

"Did they make much of a mess when they searched?" Mohal asks.

"Oh, I sorted the flat," Athena says. "And the girls tidied up Sundial."

* * *

With Nayan sprawled on the chintz sofa playing on his Nintendo, after the police visit the girls had ascended the stair case with their cleaning equipment. Rita had dusters and cloths in one hand, master keys, given to her by Athena, in the other; she noticed the Stannah stair lift has been moved from downstairs to upstairs. 'Did the police do that?' she wondered. At the top they stopped and Rita sent the lift back downstairs for any guests who need it.

Daisy and Rose at the top of the house had looked untouched. The girls gave them a quick dust and polish. Daffodil they were still reluctant to enter, as if spirits lurked there. They opened the door and went in together, leaving the door open to the corridor opposite Poppy, Marina's room. She had been away for two days on another part of her course and had missed the search. The police had left

113

the wardrobe doors open in Daffodil and Priya brushed against one of them. The girls jumped back in alarm as the empty coat hangers clanged together and started to chime like distant church bells.

"It's alright!" said Rita to calm herself and her friend. "There's nothing here." She added. They closed the doors and the drawers and wiped over the bathroom before moving to Bluebell, which felt pleasantly relaxed and untouched, and then to Poppy.

Marina's wash bag and dressing gown had been placed carefully on the bed – Rita and Priya knew they normally hang in the tiny shower room which adjoins the bedroom, so the police must have placed them there. The curtains were flung back wide – Marina usually liked to leave them half open - so the room was unusually bright. From downstairs Rita could hear the familiar sounds of Nayan congratulating himself on a football success "GOAL!" he shouted.

Marina's books had clearly been searched ('what could you hide there?' Rita thought.) They had been piled on the floor under the desk; Marina kept them on the desk, by the wall, and, in deference to her, the girls had put them back, in as best an order as they could. Rita noted that Marina was a devotee of detective fiction – she has a PD James and a Ruth Rendell in her collection alongside texts for her course and manuals and leaflets on cosmetic procedures – colonic irrigation (Yuk! thought Rita), liposuction and Botox- so maybe Marina had not given up on this as a career option? There was no evidence that Ash had spent a night there. The girls hastily completed their tidying before Marina got back to Sundial, and trailed the duster along the bannister as they went downstairs.

"Thanks, girls." Athena had said, "I'm grateful. Now the rooms will be ready for Brian's family when they come. You will stay and eat with us all on the Sunday evening?"

Rita and Priya had exchanged an alarmed look. Another meal of tension and dissension among Brian's relatives, and being careful not to mention Brian's brother, the black sheep of the family? It did not sound attractive. But they did not want to let Athena down. "Edward will be away again and Morwenna is with friends for a few days." Athena pleaded. "Of course we will." said Priya.

Chapter

13

"In people as well as plants, good and evil lie. But if the evil is more, the plant will die."

Friar Laurence in
Romeo and Juliet
by Shakespeare

Monday August 19th 2013 (early)

It is early – 9 in the morning – and there are not many people about in Abbey Park. Those who are there are mostly dog walkers or joggers, plus a small group doing Tai Chi exercises on the grass. Others are taking short cuts through the greenery. Those not involved in the ceremony cast curious glances at the group, who are all clad in white, process together to stand around a maple tree at the edge of the low abbey walls. Some of the passers-by wonder if they are making a film and look around for the cameras.

The group have permission from the City Council – they thought they should ask. The Council were reluctant at first, but the combined organising powers of Caroline and Athena were sufficient to wear them down. So they have the Council's blessing to hold a Memorial for Brian in the ruined Abbey, the place of his last performance. Caroline and Athena are the main catalysts for the gathering; they wanted to do something before the Dragon Company end their run. The tragedy of Romeo and Juliet has ended now. For the last two weeks they have been performing The Tempest instead.

The ghostly group of figures – they agreed that wearing white would be a fitting tribute - stands in two semi circles, the actors gather on one side as if for a curtain call; Alicia wears a white dress over white leggings, Caris is in a flowing white maxi dress, Judith and Rachel are in white skirts and tops, Caroline has found a smart white suit to wear for the occasion. Michael has a collarless white shirt which hangs over his beige chinos, while the other men wear ordinary white shirts but no ties, and sport jeans or black trousers. Ash has removed his woollen hat in honour of the occasion.

Brian's family are on the other side of the tree, standing in pairs. Jan, who has pearls at her neck, is next to her son, William, whom Rita has not seen before. The young man peers shyly under his fringe and is clad in a white jacket and black trousers which make him look like he is in evening dress. Brian's mother is wearing a white dress and jacket and sensible shoes, not for her the problem of stumbling over the grass in high heels, unlike some of the other women in the group. Cynthia is with Brian's mother (she thought it best not to bring Simon; he probably wouldn't understand and might get distressed). Rita and Priya, both in white salwar kameez and flat white shoes, are holding a number of balloons which will be released later. They stand with the family, alongside Athena (Morwenna is working and Edward is away again). Inspector Bridge is watching them behind sunglasses from a distance; Rita spotted him behind a tree a few metres away.

* * *

Rita recalls the evening meal at Sundial the night before. Athena's vegetable Thai curry was eaten in strained silence. Margaret was not hungry, she said it was too late to eat (it was 6.30pm) and Jan said she had got herself a sandwich and went to her room to join her son for whom she had brought in a burger ("He won't eat curry"). That left Cynthia and Simon, who tucked in appreciatively while Rita and Priya also tried to do justice to their boss's excellent cooking.

As the conversation moved to consideration of how the

ceremony would be arranged the next day, Athena raised her eyebrows to Rita and sighed. She had confided earlier, before Brian's family arrived, how much she would like to escape to the sanctuary of her flat as soon as possible. She said she valued getting away from the nervous tension around the family and the chance to meditate in the quiet. "It helps me to sleep, and to have dreams." she had told Rita.

"Dreams tell you so much." she went on, "I even had a dream that led me to buy Sundial."

Rita had been surprised at this.

"I dreamt about a sun, a clock and a pile of wood and there was a written message saying 'buy'. Then, when I looked on-line, there was this house called 'Sundial' and when I rang the agent they said it was on Woods Avenue!" Athena's face had been transported with delight as she said this, just like it must have been when she had the dream.

"So I dragged Edward to see it – he was reluctant, we'd looked at so many – and we both saw its potential straight away. The agents said maybe it would make a family home, or a small residential home, but I could see happy guests going in and out."

Rita had wished her dreams could be so vivid. Could she have a sign about which Universities to apply to please? Since she had spoken with Professor Rees she was even more confused.

Simon slipped away from the table to resume whatever he was doing on his lap top.

"I do worry sometimes," said Cynthia when he was gone, "You never know what he's up to. You read such terrible stories about boys like him accessing websites - I don't mean pornography," she added, catching a look of alarm from Priya, "I mean Intelligence and Defence websites. The Americans are very strict." ('Not that they mind invading our privacy' thought Rita, recalling a conversation with Mohal who had told her the US monitors a lot of phone calls and internet activity – 'especially if you're Asian' - in the name of preventing terrorism. His university friends had no doubt told him some of this.)

"What will happen about Simon's College place now?" Athena had asked Cynthia.

"I think that's not going to happen," Cynthia answered resignedly, helping herself to the strawberries and cream which were on offer as a desert.

"Without Brian's help we can't find the accommodation costs. It's such a shame. He'll have to live with me instead." she had said.

The conversation had turned to early memories of Brian, before he found fame as an actor.

"He stood on that picket line day after day." Margaret said proudly. "It was so cold. A cruel winter. We couldn't afford any heating. The union would give us hand-outs sometimes. People went on the coal tips looking for bits of coal to burn. The police set road blocks to stop the men picketing outside their area, so Brian stayed put and kept scabs out of Grimethorpe. They used to have a fire they stood around outside the Coal Board's offices. I look at that spot now and think what it were like." she said. Clearly the place held memories for her, even though many were sad ones. Now it will mean even more, Rita thought, a link with her dead son.

"Some men were killed on the picket line – that were in Nottingham not Yorkshire – and a taxi driver got killed in Wales taking miners to work. It was a sad time. A bad time." Cynthia added, not wanting to romanticise the strike.

"What's Grimethorpe like now?" Priya ventured to ask.

Cynthia snorted. "You wouldn't believe it." she said. "It's been designated one of the poorest areas in the EU. There's no jobs, no shops, no future really. The old Coal Board equipment has been taken away, so you get a better look at the view. It is beautiful up there, especially at sunset. But there's no future. We haven't had shops like Cortonwood have or a shopping centre like they put in to replace industry at Meadowhall in Sheffield. That's why I'd like Simon to be able to get away. To have a better life." she concluded wistfully.

* * *

Now here they are, enacting the ceremony they had talked about last night.

Caroline makes some opening remarks, ("Brian, we miss you but we want you to know you will never be forgotten.") and puts candles in a pile of sand in a box she had carried across the Park. Ash has brought an iPod dock which plays pan pipe music while they each step up to light a candle. Athena pours water over a bowl so that it keeps on flowing into the ground.

Then Jacob reads part of Prospero's speech at the end of The Tempest-

"*Our revels are now ended.*
These our actors as I foretold you were
All spirits and melted into air
Into thin air.
And like the baseless fabric of this vision,
The cloud-capped towers,
The gorgeous palaces,
The solemn temples, the great globe itself,
Yea, all that which it inherit,
Shall dissolve and,
Like this insubstantial pageant of death,
Leave not a rock behind.
We are such stuff as dreams are made on,
And our little life is rounded with a sleep.'"

Athena reads a Buddhist passage -

"*What is born will die*
What has been gathered will be dispersed
What has been accumulated will be exhausted

What has been built up will collapse
And what has been high will be brought low.'"

Rita is not really paying attention, it all seems so sad. She glances in the direction of the lake and then at Inspector Bridge, whose attention is also directed towards the lake, where Brian was found, and not towards the group.

Then Jan steps forward to the front to read a poem

"Don't cry for me now I have died, for I'm still here, I'm by your side

My body's gone but my soul is here, please don't shed another tear,

I am still here, I'm all around..."

Rita's dreaming is disturbed by Athena hissing in her ear.

"Oh no, I forgot!"

"Only my body lies in the ground" Jan says.

"Forgot what?" Rita whispers back. ('What can be so important at this moment'? she thinks)

"I am the snowflake that kissed your nose." Jan continues, looking up so see who is whispering.

"I heard someone else. Someone came in that night." Athena cups her hand to continue whispering to Rita without interrupting the poem for the others. "I was half asleep. Somehow I confused the two events. Another man and a woman, together."

Rita is feeling very confused but what can she say in the middle of the Memorial, in the middle of the crowd? She listens and pulls a puzzled face.

"I am the snowflake that nips your toes." Jan carries on steadfastly.

"He had desert boots too, but she, she..." Athena tries to explain.

Jan stops in the middle of the poem. Her face and figure are frozen. Her skin has gone as white as her clothes. She looks like an angry witch from a child's story book. Annoyance and frustration are the emotions exuding from her tight-fitting, body-hugging white dress and high heels, in a nude colour.

"Like those!" Athena points dramatically at where Jan's feet were, but the feet, with the shoes still on them, are on the move. Jan mutters something like "I'm not staying here to be insulted." And then she starts to run, insofar as she is able, towards the car park, which is on the other side of the lake.

Rita yells out, "Inspector Bridge!" towards the tree where the policeman was leaning and, letting go of the balloons she was holding, she sets off after Jan.

Priya, seeing her friend is so determined, hands her balloons to Cynthia and starts to run too, murmuring "Rita!" under her breath.

"Jan, stop!" Rita calls. The park is crowded and it is hard to pick her out – it is hard to keep up as well, as children on tricycles, adults on bicycles, dogs on leads that extend as they are walked, and every kind of obstacle, moving and stationary, seems to conspire to put distance between Rita and her quarry.

Jan turns round from time to time to see if Rita is still following. Her tight skirt and high heels are inhibiting her. She opts to walk on the grass, along the edge of the lake, and removes her shoes for speed. Priya, more athletic than Rita, is gaining on her friend and watches as the two figures of Rita and Jan get nearer to each other, and to the water.

Inspector Bridge, rounding the corner, having been alerted by Rita's shout, pauses to appraise the situation. Who is chasing who and why? Easy to make the wrong assumptions.

Then Athena is at his elbow. She is following Priya in the hope of catching sight of Rita.

"The shoes!" she says inexplicably. "Jan's shoes!" Athena takes a breath, "I saw her go into Sundial on Monday night. I forgot!" she adds.

Inspector Bridge launches into a sprint then, yelling "Stay there!" to Athena behind him and to Priya as he overtakes her. Various passers-by pause to watch the man in shorts, t-shirt and, for once, training shoes, speed across the grass, jumping over family groups who are seated on the ground as best he can, and shouting "Stop! Police!"

He is felled at last by a football lying in his path. No one could say afterwards whether the youths to whom the ball belongs had deliberately put it in his path, or whether it was just an accident. Jamie hits the ground with a thump, the wind temporarily taken out of him, his chin jarring against the hard earth.

"You alright mate?" A middle aged man comes over and tries to help him up. "Police." Jamie manages to day, his voice little more than a whisper, "Dial 999. I'm Inspector Bridge. I need a patrol car."

Jamie Bridge struggles to his feet and staggers forward, not even sure in which direction he had been running. He can hear the youths to whom the ball belongs giggling around him but he tries to blot them out. Where is Rita? Where is Jan? He wonders.

"Over here!" shouts Priya who, contrary to the Inspector's instructions, had not waited, but kept running.

Meanwhile Jan has reached the lake's edge and Rita is closing in on her. Jan stops and shouts "Leave me alone! I just want to go home!" like a tired child.

Rita keeps going until they are facing each other.

"You need to speak to the police." Rita gasps out to her, "You were at Sundial that night. You have access to drugs at the nursing home…"

"Shut up! Shut up!" the older woman rages. Rita is within touching distance now, afraid that Jan will get her second wind and run off again. Rita does not think she has the breath to keep up with her much longer.

"Come on," she says persuasively, "I'm sure there's a good reason. You need to explain."

"Good reason!" Jan explodes, "I'll say there's a good

reason. He was going to give his money to that wretched Simon, as if he could appreciate it; and he wouldn't give a bean to me or my son, William. It's so unfair! Well, I wasn't having it!"

As Rita reaches out to take Jan's arm, time stays still and everything happens in slow motion.

Athena is still standing by a tree as instructed by Inspector Bridge. Jamie Bridge is limping forward towards the lake, seeing double after his fall, his knees giving way, but determined to catch his quarry. Priya is about two metres away from the edge of the lake now and has heard some of the exchanges between Rita and Jan.

Priya watches with horror as Jan takes advantage of Rita's gesture to take her by the arm and seizes Rita's arm instead, tipping her over and into the water.

"Rita!" Priya yells and, without a thought for herself, dashes into the lake to help her friend. Jamie Bridge keeps going, ignoring the two flailing white figures in the water and finally, with a desperate lunge, he rugby tackles Jan to the ground.

The young men with the ball have followed the action and send up a cheer. "Good tackle!" they shout.

In the air, a police siren can be heard and uniformed officers start to race across the park to help Jamie Bridge. He points to the bedraggled white figures emerging from the lake, as if from a baptismal ritual, the balloons Rita had released earlier soaring into the sky above them.

"Rita." he says with all the breath he has left, "Make sure she's ok."

Chapter

14

"And thus ended the life of my late lord and master, the rich and triumphant legate and cardinal of England, on whose soul Jesu have mercy! Amen."

George Cavendish on his master
Thomas, Cardinal Wolsey

Monday August 19th 2013 (later)

The white figures make a slow pilgrimage across the Park to their vehicles and then back to Sundial. Athena insists on taking the soaked girls in her car ("There's no point getting two cars wet"). As soon as they return, Rita and Priya take showers at Athena's insistence, while she finds fresh towels and an assortment of Morwenna's clothes for them to change into.

Cynthia brings into the house a shaken Margaret ("So glad I didn't bring Simon, how would we have coped?" the ex daughter-in-law says) and pours the older woman a sherry in the sitting room - Athena had agreed they could have sherry to restore them after the Memorial.

"What does it all mean?" Margaret keeps saying. Cynthia shakes her head.

Ash comes back with various members of the cast. Marina was not at the memorial – her course finishes in a few days - and he has been trying to contact her, leaving her voicemail and text messages. Caroline, Judith reports as the sitting room fills up, has gone to the police station with Jan's son, William, to find out what is happening. Judith and Michael move to the kitchen to make tea for those who want it, noticing that the sandwiches Athena had prepared for them sit neglected in the dining room ,as the actors and the family perch awkwardly together in the sitting room and try to digest the scenes in the Park.

When Rita and Priya reappear, clad now in Morwenna's fashionable tops and leggings, they are besieged by questions.

"What did Jan say?"

"Why did she run off like that?"

"What are the police doing?"

Athena enters next and calls for quiet. "Please, everybody, let's sit down and get our breath back. I'm sure these two need some ginger tea, then we can talk." And she leaves the room to help Judith and Michael in the kitchen.

"Are you ok?" Rachel asks the girls and they nod.

"The water's not deep." says Rita.

"Even so," says Jacob with his deep voice, "Gutsy to chase after her like that."

"I had nay idea what was happening." says Ash "One minute you were there, the next you'd gone!"

"I had my eyes closed." says Alicia "When I opened them again it was all going off at the lake!"

"I couldn't move." says Caris, "It was like I was watching a play!"

"Did you see the Inspector fall over?" says Anton. "He really took a tumble! I went to help him up but an older guy got there first."

Athena re-enters with a tray of tea and some shortbread which they all devour, even Jacob takes a couple of bites; suddenly they need the comforting energy boost.

Rita and Priya, sitting alongside each other on the battered leather sofa, gratefully cup their hands round the ginger tea as their landlady stretches herself out on the floor cushions and says,

"I guess it was all my fault, really."

"How do you make that out?" says Jacob.

"I should have realised. The shoes. I suppose I was in a bit of a daze that night after my meditation." Athena expands.

"Realised what?" coaxes Cynthia who has been to check on Simon in their room; he is content on his lap top for now. "Can you explain?"

"That there were two couples who came into Sundial that night. The Monday night. The night before Brian was found. Both the men had desert boots, that's what confused me. And of course I didn't know at the time that Marina was bringing someone back." she looks up at Ash in the armchair, who looks a little shamefacedly back at her.

"But seeing Jan's shoes at the Memorial today – the nude high heels - I recalled I saw them before, on the Monday night, on the steps. But not at 11 like I thought. I think she and Brian got back about 12 or 12.30. I must have dozed off after my meditation and saw them when I woke up."

"Does that mean she killed my son?" Margaret, fortified by the sherry, asks directly.

Athena looks at Rita. "I guess it's possible. Why else would she run like that?"

Rita takes up the story, the eyes of the room turning to her.

"The police will have to sort it out," she says, "But it seems to me that now we know that Jan was at Sundial that night, it is likely she would have been responsible. She had opportunity and she had motive and means." she adds, thinking Nayan would approve of her analysis. Priya rolls her large brown eyes and reaches into the pocket of Morwenna's top where she has placed a comb. She wants to address her hair while Rita gives her explanation.

"Edward explained to me that while Jan and Brian were getting divorced, they weren't actually divorced yet. That meant that if his will left everything to Jan she would inherit; since Brian had recently come into money, after his uncle's death, it was in her interest to stop him making another will or any gifts. She didn't want him to give money to help

Cynthia's son, for example." Rita looks at Cynthia who nods. Margaret remains impassive, her face hard as a rock, not showing any emotion.

"So her motive was financial. We heard her and Brian rowing when she stayed here in May, he clearly wasn't going to give her what she wanted." Rita adds.

"She was always interested in money, that one." Margaret stirs, her top lip curling upwards in disgust.

"And how did she do it then?" Ash this time.

"Well, you heard her." Rita replies.

"Me?" Ash is puzzled.

"Mmmn. It was Jan who said 'good night Brian' – you heard that – maybe she said it loudly so you would hear. Maybe he was drugged by then. Then there was that mechanical noise. She could have taken him downstairs on the chair lift and out of the back door using the wheelchair from the hell hole – the cupboard in the hall I mean. She's stronger than she looks, and I should know!" adds Rita, ruefully recalling the way Jan had pulled her into the water.

"As long as Marina wasn't stirring – and that may be another reason she said goodnight so loudly – Jan knew there would be no one to disturb her. She'd stayed here before so she knew where everything was. I think they came back here in Brian's car and she used his car to drive them away. She probably changed him into the running clothes and put his glasses on, even though he didn't need them for running. That was a mistake." Rita adds.

"The drugs. The injection?" says Athena, her hand at her mouth, appalled.

"Well she owned a nursing home so I assume she would have access to drugs, more access than most people, and presumably enough knowledge to use them." Rita speculates.

"And where's my wheel chair?" asks Athena, still astonished.

"That may be at the nursing home too," says Rita. "Where

better to hide it?"

The phone rings then and Athena goes to answer it, returning with a sad look on her face. "That was Inspector Bridge. He confirms that Jan has confessed." she pauses. "Margaret, Cynthia, I am so sorry it turned out like this. Jan must have carried a lot of resentment. " she says, crossing the room to hug them both and producing one of her Buddhist quotes as she does so.

"Holding on to anger is like grasping a hot coal with the intent of throwing it at someone else; you are the one who gets burnt."

A few minutes later and the group are huddled together round the sandwiches in the dining room. They are like survivors of a ship wreck who do not want to let each other out of their sight. Caroline is on her way back with William who will stay with Cynthia for a few days. That evening's production of The Tempest has been cancelled. The actors and family members are chewing over the events of the morning and the revelations. In the garden they can see Simon releasing the rest of the balloons for his father's Memorial in the garden of Sundial.

When the doorbell rings, Priya opens it to admit a concerned Padma, who rushes to her daughter and friend to make sure they are alright. "Oh Rita! I thought this would be a safe job for you!" she says. Padma stays for a cup of tea and a sandwich and to be reassured that the girls are none the worse for their experience.

Then, "Come on" says Rita to Priya, picking up their wet clothes from a protesting Athena ("I can launder them for you!") as Padma indicates she is ready to take them home. "We have personal statements to finish."

Rita Patel returns in
Body in the Surgery

ISBN: 978-1-910779-72-9

ISBN: 978-1-910779-73-6

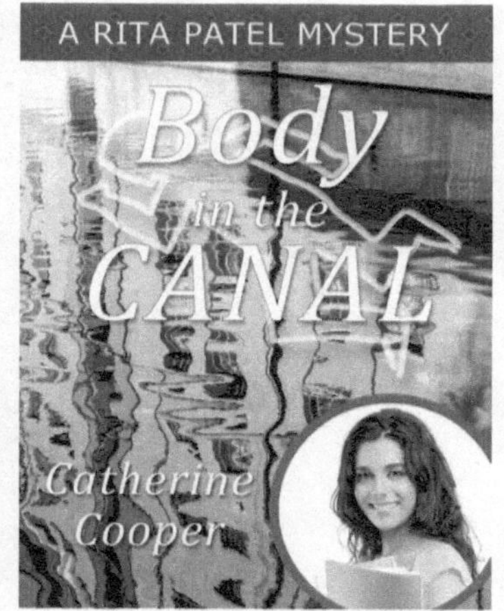

ISBN: 978-1-910779-74-3

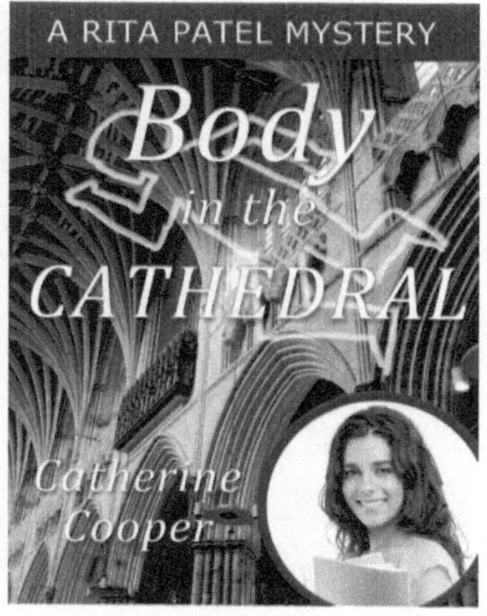

ISBN: 978-1-910779-75-0